CW00688726

THE WATCHMAN OF ROTHENBURG DIES

ADRIANA LICIO

The Home Travellers
Press

THE WATCHMAN OF ROTHENBURG DIES
A German Cozy Mystery

Book 1 in the *The Homeswappers* series
By Adriana Licio

Edition I
Copyright 2020 © Adriana Licio

All rights reserved. This book or any portion thereof may not be reproduced or used in any manner whatsoever without the express written permission of the author except for the use of brief quotations in book reviews.

This is a work of fiction. Names, businesses, places, events and incidents are either the products of the author's imagination or used in a fictitious manner. All the characters in this book are fictitious, and any resemblance to actual persons, living or dead, is purely coincidental.

Cover by **Wicked Smart Design**
Editing by **Alison Jack**

To Maria,
a best friend is the one who allows you
to "borrow" her dream dog
Napoleon, the Basset Hound also called Leon,
for writing a book

CONTENTS

1

A CHALLENGING ARRIVAL

"D o you really mean we should go through there?" Concetta Natale Passolina, known simply as Etta to her friends, stopped the old yellow Fiat 500 in the middle of the road, careless of the traffic behind them.

"That's exactly where we should go," Dorotea Rosa Pepe, or more simply Dora, insisted, pointing with her index finger to the creamy-grey stone arch that lay in front of them. "Under the arch, over the bridge, and then we're inside the old town wall."

Etta looked around in search of an 'access-denied' road sign and found none. A driver behind gently beeped their horn at them, inviting them to move on.

"Can't you see we're foreigners?" yelled Etta, waving her right arm belligerently. "Our plates are there to let you know."

The car came alongside them, and a man with white hair and an extraordinarily pale face opened the window and spoke in courteous if broken English.

"I can't speak Italian, but you can get through if you need to drop off your luggage."

"Spitalgasse?" Etta asked.

The man nodded. "Straight on." He waved at them, and then through the arch he went.

"I told you so," Dora said triumphantly. "The map is very clear – we need to go through the town's main gate, and then take the second turn on the left."

"It's so easy to know the way when you're not driving," Etta said, pushing back large glasses, their frames as red as her hair, then starting the car again and driving through the arch, still thinking there was something almost irreverent about allowing cars into the town via such a narrow passage.

"We're on a bridge! And look, there's the moat surrounding the city walls," Dora cried, clasping her hands together in wonder. "Look, over there!"

The cry made Etta jump and the car stopped abruptly as she stalled the engine. A covered wooden bridge sat on their left, affording them an almost romantic view amid lush vegetation of trees, shrubs and ivy climbing the ancient stone walls.

"I thought we had run over a tourist!" Etta said angrily. "I don't care about how pretty things are until we've arrived safely. Such a tight little bridge; I wonder what would happen if a truck came in the opposite direction."

The bridge was, in fact, much shorter than her tirade, and it led to another narrow street taking them inside the town walls.

"I hope it's large enough!" Etta tried to conceal how nervous driving through medieval European villages had made her. Her own village, Castelmezzano, way down south in Italy, was a classic example of such madness. For her entire life, she had refused to drive through its tiny alleys, steep and narrow enough to challenge even the smallest car. Those streets had been built for donkeys to pass along, in an era when cars were as fantastic a notion as teleportation is nowadays. And now, was she really supposed to drive in a village she had never been to in Germany, dating from the middle ages? Maybe Maddalena, her daughter, as awful as the notion may be, had been right for once when she'd called the whole plan madness, plain madness.

Get lost, Maddalena! Etta dismissed the thought of her bossy daughter, breathed deeply and pressed her foot down on the accelerator. Along the dark passage they went, to find themselves in a roundish courtyard. A huge oak tree shaded the area to one side and stone arches stood on the other. There were a number of tourists admiring the beauty of the scenery, enthusiastically taking pictures. But there was one more passage to go before Etta could relax too.

"I wonder where we'll end up this time!" she growled.

Dora was again clasping her hands, enraptured by the enchanting town. Her dark grey eyes dreamy, she was already in tourist heaven.

The car jolted and shuddered to a halt again. Once more, Etta switched on the engine, resolving to be more careful about the clutch and accelerator's respective positions. A few sweat droplets appeared on her forehead and she wished wholeheartedly that she'd let her friend do the driving. But then she'd only have been panicking even more than she was now. Dora would be just as enthusiastic about the scenery around her and wouldn't care less about the sides of the car hitting the narrow passageways.

Etta sighed. Squinting with eyes full of dread, she drove along the latest passage to a second courtyard, smaller than the first. Another tiny passage – well, maybe not that tiny – faced them, seeming to stretch on for ever through a tall square building made of the same creamy-grey stone as the whole town seemed to be.

As Etta's eyes searched for where the tunnel might end, Dora screamed in delight.

"This is the Spital Bastion! We're driving through its belly!"

Through the dark passage they went. Upon exiting, they felt as though they had dropped in to the *Wizard of Oz* movie when the action passes from black and white to stunning Technicolor. The relentless ochre shade had given way to two and three storey houses painted in all kinds of pastel colours: green, apricot, pale pink, light blue, yellow. From each window or balcony, a display of lively flowers spilled. The steep red roofs had nice curves, as if the women had arrived in a marzipan village, and church spires, clock towers, and delightful exposed-timber houses completed the panorama.

"Rothenburg ob der Tauber is just as pretty as they said it would be!"

"It will be even prettier when we find our accommodation, if there is any."

"Of course there is," Dora said, seriously, looking at the map she had printed from an email. "That's the bakery they mentioned, and this is where we should turn left. Please don't hit that tourist."

"There're so many of them, I don't think one less would make a difference." Etta nonetheless slammed her foot on the brake pedal with such energy that Dora's head went flying forward, then slammed back into the seat even more violently, despite the protection of the seatbelt.

"Oh my goodness!" she cried. "Fortunately, you missed him."

The Japanese tourist glared at Etta and gestured at her to be more careful. Etta wound down the car window and spoke to him, a fake smile painted on her lips.

"You'll be run over in no time if all you care about is seeing the world through the lens of your camera."

"Come on, let's concentrate on finding our home." Dora was always embarrassed by any signs of road rage. She could never understand why a perfectly normal person could turn into a furious ogre as soon as they were behind a steering wheel.

They looked around as the car moved slowly along the cobbled alley, unable to find a point of reference.

"Oh my goodness," Dora cried.

"What now? Not another Japanese tourist under my wheels?"

But Dora didn't speak. Instead, she pointed at a building with her finger. She was holding her breath, unable to utter a single word.

"Yes, that's a nice house. So what?"

"That's *our* house!" Dora finally stuttered. "It's just like it was in the pictures!"

"Really?" In fact, even Etta had to admit that the half-timbered yellow building with a little turret on the side, the roses climbing up the walls beside the main door, the wrought-iron lamps, the geraniums cascading from all the windowsills, had a heart-warming quality to move even the toughest of human beings.

"That must be our parking space," Dora added, pointing to a little gate on the side.

"Thank goodness! I won't touch this car again for the next few weeks."

Dora thought better than reminding her friend how many places they had planned to visit in the neighbourhood; they'd have enough sightseeing to do in Rothenburg for a few days at least. Smoothing out the sheet of paper on her lap, she read the instructions the Baumann family, the house owners and their first homeswap partners, had emailed.

"The keys are in the blue geranium pot beside the door," she said when the car was safely parked and Etta had joined her to take a good look at their new property. To begin with, they were more interested in taking in their surroundings than searching properly, but when they realised they had tried all of the geranium pots and found no trace of the keys, the expressions on both women's faces became somewhat more serious, and more than a little concerned.

They started removing every single geranium from its position, even the heavier pots on the windowsills.

"Maybe the keys are in the pots, beneath the soil. Let's go back to the blue one, as the instructions said," Dora suggested.

Etta dug into the soil with her usual energy. After a couple of minutes, the unfortunate plant had been extracted from its vase, its roots exposed to the light, but still no keys.

"They've forgotten to leave them!" Etta concluded bitterly. "I knew this whole homeswapping business would go wrong."

"Dieter said we could always contact him or the neighbours in case of trouble."

"No nosey neighbours, please, or they will pester us for the rest of the month. Just give our hosts a call. How could they forget to leave us the keys?"

Dora made the call, but it went straight to voicemail. She left a message in English, not yet daring to speak German. She was not as confident as Etta.

"Did we tell them the only place where there's a signal is the kitchen?" Etta enquired.

"Yes, I wrote that in the house folder. But maybe they haven't read that far."

"So they're snuggled inside our home, whilst all we have is a garden."

"But it's such a pretty garden, and there's a barbecue too."

"Yes, we can always sleep in the car and cook on the barbecue," said Etta, "for a month! Don't they have a fancy name for it nowadays? Glamping, isn't it? We've left our large house to a family of four, including two stroppy teenagers, and all we've got is a parking space and a barbecue. Maddalena will laugh out loud."

Dora looked downcast. After all, she had been the one who had insisted on trying this homeswapping thing. It'd give them the opportunity to travel for longer each time they went away, living like a local rather than staying in a commonplace hotel or B&B. Now, Etta would never forgive her. Her eyes felt watery; after three days of travelling from the Italian south, they had a right to expect some rest. They were no longer youngsters; they were two retired teachers.

"Maybe you're right, this is too adventurous for us. We

should have joined Don Peppino's bus tours to Medjugorie or Lourdes."

"That? Never!" Etta replied in horror. "We're only in our early sixties, not like the old crones who go on those kinds of trip."

"But what about Annamaria? She has joined Don Peppino's tours a number of times, and she told me how cool they are."

"Annamaria was born an old crone! Even when she was 12, she spoke like someone who was sick and tired of the world. Her idea of fun is spending the afternoon watching the washing machine spinning her laundry around."

"Hello?" A voice from the adjacent garden on the other side of a low wooden fence made them jump. "Are you enjoying Rothenburg so far?" Without waiting for an invitation, a tall, thin man with red cheeks and a little stubble on his chin stepped round and through the gate to shake hands with them.

"The nosey neighbour!" Etta whispered. Dora shushed her promptly.

"What?" the man asked, his grey eyes sparkling behind the small glasses perched on his nose.

"Nothing, she was just reminding me of something." Out of necessity, Dora found the courage to practise the German she had brushed up on at home. "I'm Dora and this is my friend Etta. We're homeswapping with Dieter Baumann and his family."

"You speak German? This is a nice surprise. My wife Marie will be very pleased; she's not too confident with her English."

"We're both language teachers, though I've not been practising my German too much…"

"Your German is excellent," said the man in his pleasant, soothing voice. "I'm Joseph, your neighbour. Dieter sent us a message to say that they really love both your house and your village in the south of Italy. They sent us a few pictures too."

"Of course they like it, they have a roof over their heads," murmured Etta.

"And you, do you like their house?" he asked kindly. "It's one of the oldest buildings in Rothenburg."

"Yes, we like it, but actually, we rather hoped to get inside," Etta replied.

The man looked at them without understanding. "Have you had a look around, or have you just arrived?"

"We've just arrived," said Dora, showing him the printed email. "And, in fact, we haven't been able to find the keys. They were supposed to be in the blue geranium pot."

Joseph looked at the email, read through it, then smiled at them. "It says the blue geranium pot by the back door. This is the front door, and they always keep the keys on the other side of the house."

He led them around the back of the house and went straight to a blue ceramic vase, lifting the inner pot and showing them the keys. Both women went crimson, and Etta gave Dora a hard look. She pretended not to notice.

"We all know they keep them here. Rothenburg is a pretty safe place, you know. We tend to leave our doors unlocked, at least if we'll only be out for a short while."

He opened the door and showed them in. The living room was enchanting, full of light with a characteristic beamed ceiling, a few suspended wrought-iron lamps, and large leaded windows sharing a common windowsill, on which stood a variety of pots and plants in all shapes and sizes. An old ebony table stood in the middle of the room, and to the side, a green sofa was facing a *stube* covered with pastel-green majolica tiles, a wooden bench all around it adorned with colourful pillows.

"Such a cosy corner," Dora cried, already forgetting her recent despair and eyeing the books on the bookshelf.

"I'll show you the rest of the house," and Joseph led them through a kitchen with a chequered black-and-white floor, then up a creaky wooden staircase to their bedrooms and a large bathroom, an old-fashioned bathtub with clawed feet and brass taps taking pride of place. He turned to them from time to time to make sure they appreciated what they were seeing. And Etta did; she couldn't stop grinning. The house was more than satisfactory. She had been certain this homeswapping scheme was nothing but a new form of scam; she had only agreed to it so that Dora could see that with her own eyes and they could put an end to this nonsense once and for all. But maybe she had been wrong, for once.

The man showed them where they could find spare towels and linen, and the dark, spooky basement that housed home-made apple juice, fruit preserves and sauerkraut beside the washing machine and dryer.

On the kitchen table lay the folder with all the house instructions, a pile of tourist brochures, and a personal list of favourite walks, shops, bakeries and restaurants in the area.

"So, do you like the house?" Joseph asked them again. He really seemed to care, as if it was his own house and he had a duty to make sure the two women had the best experience ever.

"It's pretty indeed, and we will love our stay here," Dora said, clasping her hands together, her cheeks seeming plumper than ever as she giggled. "You see, it's our first homeswap, and I don't think we could have found a better place to start."

Joseph eyed Etta too. She was trying to withhold her true feelings a bit, for no better reason than to balance out Dora's enthusiasm, but even she had to nod in approval. They could relax in the garden in the afternoons, walk and do touristy things in the mornings, and maybe – just maybe – drive out to explore the places in the surrounding area, too.

"Do you want me to help you with the luggage?" the man asked.

"Don't you worry," said Dora.

"Yes, please," said Etta at exactly the same moment.

Two minutes later, Joseph was wondering how it was possible to stuff an apparently tiny Fiat 500 with so many pieces of luggage. OK, there was a roof box, but still, it was a Fiat 500's roof box. Some stuff he left in the kitchen; the two women had done their grocery shopping on the outskirts of Rothenburg, guessing they wouldn't find a supermarket within the old city walls. Then he carried two large suitcases upstairs, along with a small but very heavy bag containing books, and a few more pieces of luggage of indeterminate purpose.

Cloaked in sweat from the effort, but still kind and smiley, he extended an invitation.

"Would you join us for a simple dinner tonight? My wife, Marie, would be very happy to get to know you. She's in love with Italy and all things Italian."

"Tonight?" Etta replied, her tone guarded. "We're meant to go on the Night Watchman Tour of Rothenburg tonight. My daughter, Maddalena, bought us the tickets."

"I see, but the tour won't start before half past nine. If you're not too tired, you could join us in our beer garden at 6.30pm, and we'll have plenty of time for eating and chatting before the tour. It starts in the Market Square, Rothenburg's main square, which is only a ten-minute walk from here."

"Beer garden sounds good to me," Etta declared. Dora nodded, and the man left with the invitation to call him should they need any help.

"A nice neighbour," Dora commented.

"Much better than Zia Carmela next door to us," Etta conceded.

"Hopefully she won't give our guests a hard time."

"I might decide to do her in if she does."

"But the house – isn't it pretty? And I can't wait to see the rest of the village."

"I can't wait to unpack and have a shower; it's been a long drive."

"Ah yes, we'd better get started soon if we're really supposed to eat our dinner at 6.30."

"Such a strange time for a dinner," Etta agreed. It was rare back home to eat their dinner before half-past eight or even nine o'clock in the evening. "I mean, the sun is still high. Germans are strange."

"Maybe strange, but very kind," Dora added, as ever trying to please as many people as she could at once. "We've just arrived and we've already got an invitation to dinner. It's as the Home Swapping Circle International's President said: it's not only about saving on the cost of a hotel; you'll get to experience places from a different point of view, too."

2

A GERMAN DINNER

"Joseph told me you arrived in a Fiat 500." Marie was a middle-aged woman with a tanned face, straight blonde hair parted on the side, and heavy-lidded light-blue eyes, but it was her huge winning smile that made Etta and Dora feel instantly at ease.

"It's such a pretty antique car," Joseph commented.

"It's not an antique! It's Dora's car, and always has been since she learned to drive." Etta, being older than her friend's car, didn't appreciate the Fiat being referred to as if it were an ancient relic.

"And what is your job?"

"I'm... I was an English teacher. I retired this year, the same as Dora."

"And are you sisters?"

"Not at all, just colleagues."

"Yes, I was a French teacher," Dora said with a certain pride.

"And how come you can both speak German so well?"

"I lived in Germany with my husband for three years," Etta spoke fast; she wanted to get this part of the conversation over and done with as soon as possible, although she knew it was unavoidable, "when our daughter was young, before we divorced and I moved back to Castelmezzano. I've lived there ever since."

"My German is not as fluent as Etta's," Dora explained. "But when I was young, in summer, I would accompany a group of mothers and children to join their husbands who were working in Frankfurt. I picked up a little German on those occasions."

"We also studied German at school, alongside English and French, and I kept it up." Etta didn't add that her greatest fear was to be afflicted by a loss of memory of any sort, so she was a strong believer that exercising her brain was important, otherwise, like any other muscle, it would lose its ability. Her doctor had explained to her that often diseases associated with old age didn't just happen because of a lack of 'exercise', but his stubborn patient had pooh-poohed his explanation, so he thought there was no harm in letting her believe what she wanted. And actually, some good would probably come out of it.

"And in whose house is Dieter staying with his family?"

"Our house." Dora was happy to give their hosts a full explanation, going into detail if needed. "You see, after we retired, we had this great dream of travelling. But taxes are so awfully high, and a teacher's pension doesn't amount to much. There's maybe just enough to keep a roof over one's head and scrape a living."

"But no way could we enjoy travel of any sort," Etta continued. "Homes are so expensive to maintain. It was then we decided that if we shared a home and a car, we'd be able to share all the expenses, too. And that would leave us enough money to travel a bit."

Dora giggled. "Then a friend mentioned this idea of homeswapping…"

"It fitted our plans perfectly as it would allow us to take longer trips than a conventional holiday."

"And we could avoid using aeroplanes, as Etta is not too fond of flying…"

"I don't think humans were meant to fly. Otherwise we'd

ADRIANA LICIO

have been born with wings," Etta said stiffly. She didn't like her
weaknesses to be common knowledge.

"And is this your first homeswap?" Marie asked, curious.

The two of them nodded in approval. "It is."

"Dieter sent me a few photos through WhatsApp of your
village and home. It looks like a fairy-tale place, perched up on
the mountains."

Both Dora and Etta were proud of Castelmezzano and its 800
souls, and gladly accepted all the compliments on its behalf.
They had secretly feared Dieter's family might find their stay in
such a small place rather dull and were relieved to discover that
wasn't the case.

"They say the local people are so friendly, there's plenty of
sightseeing around, and the weather's always sunny and warm."

"Glad to hear they're enjoying it," Dora admitted. "But
Rothenburg looks like a fairy tale too."

"You probably haven't had time today as you've been busy
settling in, but you'll see it better tomorrow. It's such a quaint
little town."

"We're actually going to discover a bit of it tonight," Dora
said, her hair with its salt-and-pepper fringe flicking around her
plump face as it did whenever she was enthusiastic about
something.

"My silly daughter," Etta continued, "has booked us a tour
this very night with the Night Watchman. We would rather have
relaxed tonight and gone on another day, but she'd already
booked us the tickets."

"Ah yes, the 9.30 tour from the Market Square," Marie
confirmed. "Our son Johannes leads a similar tour, but the
Tourist Bureau only sponsors the Night Watchman, so I'm afraid
he gets all the glory... and the tourists, too. But here comes
Johannes now." She pointed at a lanky man in his mid-twenties
who was coming into the garden just then. He was as tall as his
father, but apart from that, he was a carbon copy of his mother.
The same bony face, blond hair, slightly drooping eyelids, a

14

scattering of freckles across his nose, and the same generous, smiling mouth.

Marie made the introductions, then Johannes asked the two friends about their village back in Italy. As he spoke, he had a tendency to blush, but Etta and Dora could see how eager he was to get to know new people – even two elderly ladies – so he was striving to overcome his shyness.

A table had been laid outdoors with a light-blue cloth and white porcelain dishes. Some roundish jars with a tea candle in each were hanging all around the porch as lanterns. Even though the evening this far north was still bright, the candles gave the garden a warm and welcoming atmosphere.

"This is so pretty," cried Dora, ever the romantic, her slate grey eyes shining like the flickering candles.

"We'd better get started," said Marie, inviting them to take a seat. "Johannes, these two ladies are planning to join the Night Watchman's tour tonight. It was booked by Etta's daughter."

"Oh, I'm sorry," Etta said, seeing the smile disappear from the young fellow's face. "We didn't know our neighbour's son would be offering the same kind of tour or we would have booked with you."

"You can have another tour with Johannes while you're here," said Joseph calmly. "He'll be happy to be your guide over the next few days."

"We'd love that for sure," said Dora with a smile.

"The Night Watchman is a surly old man," said Johannes, a shade of harshness in his voice. "I don't think you'll enjoy that tour much; he delves too much into history, but people prefer funny anecdotes about the old town, how people lived, what was comfortable and what was not. There's so much to tell them; Rothenburg is full of legends and quirky places."

"I'm sure you do all that very well with your own tours," Dora said.

"Not with that man being the only official Night Watchman." Johannes sighed. "I'd love to offer my tour under the same name and get a bit more recognition, but tourists simply find Sebastian's tours on the Tourist Bureau website and book him up. We – all the other night guides – are left almost empty-handed."

"Maybe you should speak to him," Dora suggested. "Older people are often only too pleased when someone offers to carry on their work."

"Oh no, he'd not be pleased at all," explained Johannes, slowly scooping out a serving of mushroom and potato soup. "He guards his position with all his might; he doesn't like competition of any sort. And he would do anything to expel me from the town."

At that moment, the phone rang and Johannes went to pick up the call.

"Is it really that bad? Maybe we shouldn't go on the tour," Dora said.

Marie looked mortified. "Oh, not at all, I'm sorry if we've ruined your expectations. But it's an old story. Johannes and Charlotte, his fiancée, plan to get married in a year or so. Charlotte helps her grandma run the souvenir shop, and the two young ones want to take it on full time, but it's in a more hidden part of the town. If Johannes could have a few happy customers on his tour, he could encourage them to visit the shop and create another viable income stream. Sebastian Sauer, the Night Watchman, has been doing the job for so long, he's surely due to retire and leave the way clear for the youngsters. He's already in his sixties, so it's not as essential for him to build a career as it is for younger people. But he won't step aside. He gets completely unreasonable if anyone suggests it."

Marie left to go into the kitchen, and came back with a tray of pork tenderloins, served with plenty of vegetables on the side.

"This is a cranberry sauce to go with the meat," she said, passing around a white gravy boat. "It's a Franconian speciality."

"The meat melts in the mouth," said Dora, a keen cook

herself, trying to guess how it had been seasoned. As she and Marie discussed the best cuts of meat, and the herbs and spices that complemented the different cuts, Etta's thoughts wandered. Etta loved good food when it was served to her, but her cooking skills went no further than freezer to microwave. Until a few weeks earlier when Dora had joined her in her Castelmezzano house, the only time she ate fresh food was when she visited a restaurant. She couldn't care less which cut of pork was better than another for a particular dish, and so it was that Etta's keen ears picked up Johannes's tone of voice as he spoke on the phone. She couldn't make out the words he was saying, but the disappointment in his voice was clear.

When the young man came back, his large smile had vanished.

"Are you going to pick Charlotte up?" his mother asked.

"No," he said, sinking into his chair. "She just phoned to say they're running late, and once she's done, she'd rather go straight home. She feels tired."

"Charlotte," Joseph explained, "entered the Rothenburg Theatre Company this spring, and they're now rehearsing for their first ever play."

"And men always find it hard to put up with their women having a busy life if it doesn't include them," Marie teased Johannes.

"Mum, that's not fair," he protested, his face still sombre, and then he sighed. "It's not that; I'm so happy she overcame her shyness to go into acting. It is just that… just that…"

His mother smiled at him encouragingly as the young man looked like an adolescent coming to terms with the strange ways in which life proceeds.

"She's changed. She's not like she used to be. She no longer laughs at my jokes, we don't go for long walks or bike rides and discuss our future plans anymore. It's like… like she's moving away from me."

"Oh, you silly man," his mother roughed up his hair, "it's an important time for her. There are so many emotions being stirred up for her by being part of the theatre, and she works full time with her granny at the shop. You'll see – after the play's opening night, things will go back to normal."

Johannes didn't reply, but a shy smile flashed across his face.

Turning towards her guests, his mother added, "I can't wait for you to meet Charlotte, she's a sweetheart really. And her souvenir shop is a place you shouldn't miss in Rothenburg."

"I'm impatient to visit the town and its shops," said Dora with such excitement, it sent shivers down Etta's spine. They certainly couldn't waste all their money on souvenirs, but Dora went on, carefree as usual. "And you, Johannes, do you help in the shop too?"

"Yes, I do. That is, when I get a little time between tourist tours and the Crime Museum's outdoor exhibition that I'm involved in right now."

"That's a lot to do!" Dora cried.

"Well, in such a small town, we need to be jacks of all trades and pass from one job to another according to the season."

"And now the dessert," said Marie. "I've had no time to bake anything, but I'm sure Joseph picked up something nice at his favourite cake shop." And she opened a box to extract a deep, dark and shining chocolate cake.

"Is that a *sachertorte*?" Etta asked.

"Actually, no," said Joseph. "But as you're the guest, you can cut the first slice."

Etta took up the knife and approached the cake with such a murderous look on her face, Dora halted her.

"Please, stop there," she cried at full volume. "I'm sure you'll kill that poor cake and send it flying all over the garden."

Etta wore her most sulky expression. She knew she didn't have Dora's culinary talents, but there was no need to let the whole of Rothenburg know about it. Nonetheless, when Dora cut the first slice, she found herself clapping her hands and stamping her feet along with Marie and her family.

When Dora laid that first slice in a dish, it revealed at least seven layers of thin white sponge, just as many layers of chocolate buttercream contrasting with them.

"This is the Bavarian *prinzregententorte!*" Marie exclaimed. "Impossible not to love it, but you're right – there are some similarities between it and the *sachertorte*, as the last layer is a bonus of apricot jam."

Silence fell around the table as they all savoured the cake, until Dora giggled.

"At least we managed to avoid this delicious treat being murdered," she said, and they all laughed. Except for Etta.

3

THE NIGHT WATCHMAN'S TOUR

Just after nine o'clock, Dora and Etta left their home. It still wasn't dark, but yellow light from the town's old lamps was spilling over the paved road that led to the belly of the Siebers Tower.

"It's so nice to enter a tower walking rather than driving, it feels so comfortably roomy," Etta said pragmatically. The less practical Dora clasped her hands as she did every time she felt overwhelmed by something beautiful – which occurred far too often, according to Etta.

"It's *sooo* romantic," she said with a giggle. "And a little spooky – the perfect place for fairy tales. We really are on the Romantic Road."

They walked past the tower, only to turn back at the tourists around them shouting in wonder and taking pictures. They were at the Plönlein Fork, each street graced with a clock tower and a plethora of beamed houses. One of them, just above the fork itself, looked as if it was suspended between the main road and the one going down towards the Kobolzeller Tower and Gate. In its pointy, curvy roof, a row of four windows had such skewed profiles that no two lines in the whole building had the perfectly straight geometry of a modern construction. With the lamps lit in the windows showing bookshelves and beamed ceilings inside the rooms, with a gilded bell in a wrought-iron shop sign sparkling in the lamplight, they really seemed to have entered a picture postcard.

Dora stopped, unable to move on. She opened her eyes, then closed them for a few seconds.

"Are you feeling sick?" Etta asked her.

"No," she protested. "I'm trying to imprint this image upon my memory. I want to remember it forever…"

"Can't you do that tomorrow, when we're in less of a hurry?"

"I want to do it now, before we get so used to it that we no longer notice."

"Can't you do as we all do?" Etta shrugged impatiently. "Shoot it with a camera and have it impressed in your memory card? It takes two seconds, and if it works for the Japanese, it will work for you too."

"It's not the same, I want an *internalised* picture."

"And I recommend having an *external* back-up, just in case."

Dora shook her head and they both moved on, though not as fast as Etta would have wished. Along the Schmiedgasse, there were more stone portals, more shop windows, more cute corners and more views. In the end, Etta had simply to drag her friend all the way up to the Market Square. Once they were there, before Etta had even had the time to look around, Dora gave her umpteenth cry of joy at the sight of the square. Etta snorted rebelliously, although even she had to admit to herself that the sight was remarkable.

The porched Rathaus looked as if it was a piece of refined embroidery, and all around the square were clocks, towers and spires in every size and shape. The beamed buildings, with their pointed roofs standing against an extraordinary blue sky that was finally slipping in to darkness, would have moved even the most unromantic of souls.

They stood there, letting it all sink in. It was then that Dora saw it: a black shape against the bare stone wall just beside them.

It was still, looking like a bat resting head downwards for the night.

"Oh my goodness, what's that?" she cried, attracting the attention of the tourists all around. Slowly two wings unfolded and, in a rather theatrical movement, a tall and extraordinarily thin man emerged from a dark cloak. He was holding a halberd and a lantern that seemed too heavy for him, a horn hanging from his neck curving his shoulders inwards, the Rothenburg coat of arms on his sunken chest. When he raised his head, a devilish smile crossed his cadaverous face and dark, malicious eyes sparkled under the lamplight.

"Welcome to Rothenburg, I'm the Night Watchman of this charming city. And as you're about to discover, it wasn't always such a romantic place as you might imagine. Dark deeds occurred between these harmless and sweet marzipan buildings."

The gathered tourists all giggled, shivers of pleasure running down their backs.

Next to the Night Watchman at ground level, something moved amongst the folds of his cloak. Something was trying to make its way through – something pointed.

Gasps of terror came from the crowd. Even the Night Watchman looked stunned.

More convulsions came from beneath the cloak, then finally a nose emerged. Then a whole head with long ears, and finally, inch by inch, the body of a dog made its way through.

"A Basset Hound!" cried one of the tourists.

"Napoleon, what are you doing here?" the Night Watchman cried. Then he turned to the tourists. "This naughty beastie never does as he is told."

Napoleon barked in protest at being called a naughty beastie.

"We'd run too late if I were to take him back home. Anybody wish to take care of him as we go exploring?"

Dora immediately raised her hand, as did a man in the crowd.

"You make your choice, Leon," the Night Watchman said.

The Basset Hound without hesitation moved towards Dora.

"Sorry, my man, but he prefers women." The Night Watchman grinned and made a slight bow at Dora. "And you can take him home with you, too. I have had enough of him stealing my sausages and chewing my socks."

"This cute doggy? I'd never believe that," Dora said as Napoleon sat in front of her, his head tilted and the most endearingly frantic expression in his round brown eyes.

Etta sent Dora a dirty look. She didn't like pets at all, not even outside. Cuddly toys were fine, but not real animals, the smelly, dirty things, raising their legs and peeing everywhere, shedding hair as if there were no tomorrow. That was something she would never put up with.

"Time to move on, otherwise our tour will never end, and I need beer – soon. Have I told you what an important job mine was? In the middle ages, what people feared more than pestilence and superstition were the Turks and the fire. And who could save them from both? Only me, the Night Watchman of Rothenburg."

He winked at a woman with a round body and the nicest smile on her pretty face.

"Would you hold this for me?" he said, holding out his lamp.

"Certainly," the woman said, stretching out her hands to take it.

"Such a sweetie! And would you marry me, too?"

General laughter.

"Only don't tell my wife." The rascal lit the lamp and took it back from the woman. "We will discuss the particulars when these curious folks have left us in peace."

He raised both his lamp and his voice and spoke to the whole group.

"As usual, my beloved citizens, filled with all kinds of jealousies, wouldn't admit how important I was for the community. To their silly eyes, I was only marginally more important than the gravedigger."

There was more laughter as the Night Watchman talked of superstitions and black magic and beliefs of the middle ages.

~

AFTER A TOUR THROUGH ROTHENBURG'S DARK ALLEYS, PASSING hidden monuments and apparently peaceful churches, the tour group arrived back in the main square. The Night Watchman stopped in the northern part of the square and spoke in a conspiratorial voice, his eyes darting around.

"But silence, now, because I was not the only one who saved Rothenburg from certain death."

He waited for something to happen, his hand cupping his ear as if to catch a distant sound. The group watched with bated breath, their eyes wandering around the square, waiting for something terrible to happen.

Then the clock chimed.

The Watchman pointed up to the clock on the white building in front of them and invited his guests to watch as two small windows opened up and two figures appeared. One was a noble knight, and the other a simple man dressed in black. The latter took a giant tankard to his lips and, in a single long gulp, drank and drank and drank.

After the last chime, the Watchman told them the story of the Meistertrunk, the Master Draught, who during the Thirty Years' War saved Rothenburg from certain destruction by winning his bet to drink a whole gallon of wine in a single gulp. The promise was that if he managed the legendary challenge, not a single stone of his dear city would be touched. And impressed, the leader of the conquerors, General Tilly, kept his word.

The group toured through the cobbled streets and narrow alleyways, Napoleon enjoying all Dora's pats on his head and looking at Etta with a resentful glare. If she didn't like him, he didn't like her either. The hound certainly didn't lack in character. One of the men in the group tried time and time again to pat him too energetically for his tastes, and kept referring to him as a perfect Hush Puppy. Napoleon stood stoically patient, taking the comparison to a pair of shoes on the chin, bearing all the unpleasantness, biding his time until the man was looking up at one of the aristocratic buildings on the elegant Herrngasse. Then he sniffed the man's trousers, raised his leg and…

"What the heck?" the tourist cried in anger.

People laughed, silently at first, then more and more loudly. Napoleon's victim protested at full volume, but when he realised sympathy was in short supply, he stormed off and left the group without saying goodbye.

"Leon!" The Night Watchman went to face the dog fiercely. "We've lost a paying customer! No steak for you tonight."

Leon pressed his chin to the ground, sliding his nose between his paws as if to say, "I'm sorry."

"Ahh," the people protested in sympathy.

"That man clearly provoked him," Etta said. Despite not liking the beast, she always made it her priority to be fair in life.

"But he was a paying customer! Am I not putting up with you all despite your foibles? Even that troublemaker of a child?" The Watchman pointed to a young boy, who had been spoiling the tour with his loud cries and speaking over the guide's words. "But I guess one's job is one's job, and after all, the customers are always right – almost."

More laughs as the child's mother turned crimson and, for the first time, urged her son to be quiet.

"I'm only joking," the Night Watchman apologised to the woman, "and mostly, I hope you won't run away without paying for your tickets as the gentleman before you did. Because, you see, we're almost at the end of our tour."

They were at the far end of the Herrngasse. In front of them stood yet another imposing tower, this one part of the fortified city walls. In keeping with Rothenburg's other towers, people could pass through its belly, but before they could enter this one, the Watchman stopped the group.

"The passage is narrow. Well, it is if you're driving a large car, anyway, and it's filled with the unexpected, so don't cram in all together. Take your time, and look out on your right for the ancient wooden door panel. It used to be shut at night time, and you'll see carved in it a much smaller door. If they were admitted within the city walls at night, people could enter only one at a time, and they had to bend to pass through – a position from which it'd be hard to attack a guard. People were smart in those times, and mostly they were expecting the worst to happen.

"Once you're out of the tower on the other side, turn back and look above your heads. You'll see a smiling mask from which soldiers could gently pour hot oil and burn alive anyone trying to attack the town. I'm telling you, they were nice folks in those times. Enter at your own pace, and risk. I'll be waiting for you on the other side."

And before disappearing into the dark corridor, he turned to deliver one more warning.

"Beware, this town is not as it seems."

Slowly the group moved into the semidarkness and looked for the small wooden door on the right. It was so little, it seemed that only a child could squeeze through. Photos were being photographed, shots shot, flashes flashed, laughter laughed, when all of a sudden Leon let loose a long, mournful howl and pulled forward. Dora almost fell over as she tried not to let go of the leash.

As Leon continued pulling beyond all resistance, Dora had to run after him through the tower on to the bridge, Etta following close behind, then out into a park, mostly in complete darkness. Leon kept running as if he was possessed; he didn't stop until he reached a certain point in the garden outside the city walls, then he stuck his nose into what looked like a heap of clothes and released another howl that sent shivers through the spines of his two pursuers.

4

THE CORPSE IN THE GARDEN

"What's this?" Dora asked, her eyes struggling to get used to the darkness.

As soon as Etta switched on her mobile phone torch, the two women's voices harmonised in one single powerful scream. Then Etta had second thoughts and cut her ululation short.

"It must be some sort of joke. This moron will stop at nothing to give us the shivers with his ghost tour."

"It isn't a ghost tour, it's a Night Watchman's tour," Dora specified.

"Whatever!" Etta said. Stretching her hand out, she shook the figure on the ground vigorously. "Come on, stop messing around and get up!" Then doubt fell over her all of a sudden. She touched the body's neck to check his pulse. There was none.

"I think he might really be dead." Then Etta yelled in the direction of the tower passage, "Help, help, HELLLP!"

A few people from their group ran over and joined them.

"What's happened?" Someone shone a torch in their direction, and in the light, they saw the Rothenburg Night Watchman lying on the ground, a halberd planted in his chest, his legs wide apart, the broken lamp a few steps away where it had landed, and a strange iron mask that appeared to have rolled over to nestle close to the corpse.

"Is it a joke?" one asked.

Etta shook her head. "The last laugh is on him. I think he's dead. Can you call the police?"

WHEN THE POLICE ARRIVED, THEY FOUND THE WHOLE GROUP OF tourists around the corpse, each of them trying to explain what had happened. A domineering chief inspector took control, looking at his sergeant and telling her to ensure nobody left the area, but to move them towards the other side of the park which was illuminated by lamplight.

"Madam, you should leave the crime scene too and join the others," the chief said to Dora. "You can't stay so close to the body."

"But Leon refuses to come away." Dora pointed to the Basset Hound who was lying on the ground beside his master, despite all her solicitations. "He's his dog."

The chief inspector reached out to grab Leon's collar with his hand and shoo him away, but a deep growl made him think again.

"We'll have to sedate him," he said. "Sergeant, call the dog shelter. And you two, move away."

"I'm not leaving poor Leon to go to any shelter." Dora's plump face was red with anger. "His owner entrusted him to me, and I will return him to his family."

"Sauer has… I mean, had no family," the chief inspector replied drily. "Anyway, as you're here, you can tell me who found the body. The man who phoned us?"

"It was the dog," Dora answered, leaving him befuddled.

Etta realised she'd better explain what had happened. By the time she'd finished, the chief was ready with more questions.

"Could anybody within your group have reached the man before you did?"

"I don't think so. Dora and I were at the head of the group, and the others were lagging behind, waiting to take pictures of the tower passage and the small wooden door inside."

"Are you sure?"

Dora and Etta looked at each other, reconstructing the moment.

"Everything happened rather fast. As we reached the tower, Leon howled and ran away. Nonetheless, I'd say no one went ahead of us."

"Did you hear anything suspicious?"

"No," said Etta, and Dora shook her head in agreement.

"But something alerted the dog if, as you say, he ran towards his master."

"Maybe," admitted Etta, "he heard something that we simply didn't catch."

"And animals can sense things we can't," Dora added, bending down to the dog, trying fruitlessly to persuade him to leave his master.

"Did you see anything at all?"

"Well, it was pretty dark, so no, we didn't see anything much, apart from Leon lying next to the body. I didn't even realise it was a body until Etta switched on her mobile phone's torch."

Having overseen the shepherding of the tour group to the other side of the gardens, the sergeant had joined her chief inspector and the two women. Now, she looked up.

"There should have been a lamp on here, too, like the one on the other side of the Castle Gardens." She moved her flashlight and highlighted a pole. It was indeed very close to them, but the light was off.

"Do you think he stumbled on to his own halberd?" Dora asked the sergeant, who was more civil than the chief.

"I don't think so. He's lying chest up."

"Oh my goodness, do you mean he was murdered?"

"I couldn't possibly say until…"

The sergeant's response was interrupted by the arrival of the scene-of-crime team. As the chief inspector talked to them, the sergeant addressed Dora.

"Now, we really have to get the dog away from the crime scene before they can get to work."

Dora begged, pulled, shouted. Leon remained indifferent.

"Etta, please help me lift him," she said finally.

"I'm not touching that dirty drooling thing. So what if he's a faithful animal? Let the police deal with him."

"They will call the dog shelter! The poor dear is in shock; imagine how he'll feel if he's dragged away and put in a cold cage all alone."

Etta looked at Leon. She'd never realised an animal could feel pain and sorrow the way humans did, but something in the dog's face struck her and moved her more than she'd like to confess.

"What if he bites me? He's already growled at the inspector."

"He won't bite us," Dora stated with conviction.

Etta sighed. "Where do we start? He's so long."

"You take the bum, I'll take the head – the part with the teeth."

Leon let out a little whine. Rigid as a stockfish, he was carried over to where the rest of the group stood. His nose still pointed in the direction of his master, his body trembled and shivered. It took some effort, but in the end, Dora sat him on her lap on a bench and cuddled him.

"Who could imagine a dog could be this heavy?" Etta commented, patting the sweat from her forehead. For a few minutes, all attention was on the dog, with people caressing him and murmuring comforting words to him as if they were more sorry for him than the poor Night Watchman. Then the sergeant and a colleague came over and started taking statements and contact addresses from each of them, asking when they planned to leave Rothenburg.

"You cannot leave town until we give you permission," she said. As a chorus of protests rose, she added, "But I've taken down the names and contact details of those of you who are meant to leave tomorrow, and we'll make sure to speak to you first thing in the morning. If we don't need any more from you, you will be free to go. But I can't tell you more until we've spoken to the forensics and have a better picture of the crime."

The sergeant counted them again, checked their names on her list, and one by one let them go. Finally, only Etta, Dora and Leon remained, all sitting on the bench.

"Do you want me to call the animal shelter now? I think he's calmed down a bit," the sergeant said, gently stroking the dog's head.

"No way," said Dora.

"Yes please," said Etta at the same moment.

"I will leave you a few minutes to decide," the sergeant said, glancing over at the crime scene, "but I think it'd be good for Leon to stay in a proper home rather than at the shelter, at least for tonight."

"Of course," said Dora. "Etta, I will not hear of such a thing. Leon is coming with us."

"He will never come along," protested Etta. "And we can't drag him all the way home."

"Then I will carry him all the way in my arms."

"You will break your back! Don't forget, we're not that young any longer."

"Then I'm sure he will follow us now."

Etta realised it was time to call on her full artillery or everything would be lost to the furry beast. "May I remind you, Miss Dorotea Rosa Pepe," she said in a grave tone, "that when we decided to move in together under the same roof, we signed a contract stating that no furry thing of any sort, not even a taxidermied one, would ever be allowed in our house?"

The artillery was doomed to failure.

"That was an extortion, not a contract," Dora replied icily.

"But it's not even our own house," Etta implored, changing tactics. "We can't take a drooling, peeing beast to our kind hosts' house."

"Really? I could swear I saw a couple of bowls in the kitchen, and I've seen plenty of pictures around the house. I'm sure they used to have a dog."

"Let's send him to the shelter for tonight, then we'll talk to them tomorrow, and if they say it's OK, we'll go and see how the dog is doing."

Leon placed his large paw on Dora's knee as she had stopped tickling him under the ears. It was the first time the dog had done anything that didn't involve beseeching them to let him return to his master and Dora's heart melted instantly.

"Then I'll book a room in a hotel."

It was rare that Etta couldn't find the words to express how she felt, but none came out of her mouth now. She was flabbergasted. She had known Dora for 50 years or more and had always considered her a quiet, meek woman, even a bit of a pushover, whose will she could command and influence to her own. Now all of a sudden, she'd discovered there was a real mule inside the woman, a stubborn creature over which she held no power whatsoever. Something told her that the battle was lost and she'd better accept the fact for the night.

"OK, let's drag the dog home, but if he runs away and gets hurt, or if he pees or messes in the house, I will not be held responsible."

5

A LONG WAY HOME

I t wasn't an easy walk. Leon was unwilling to follow them, every so often sitting down and refusing to move, his bum seeming to increase its weight by a few hundred kilos. No amount of dragging, imploring or pulling would work.

Etta entered a pub and begged the first member of staff she encountered to fetch her a würstel from the kitchen.

"But the kitchen is closed," the officious waiter replied, looking at his watch. "At this time of night, we only serve drinks."

"I don't need you to cook it. Frozen, raw or rotten – anything will do."

The waiter looked at her in shock. "Are you homeless?" he asked.

"I will be soon if you don't help me out."

The man disappeared into the kitchen and came back with a würstel on a plate.

"It's cold from the fridge, should I microwave it?"

"Nope," and she dropped a two euro coin on the counter and left, grabbing the würstel with her bare hand. But when the dog turned his nose up at the sausage and fixed his sad, watery eyes on the middle of her face, as if asking, "Do you really think a stupid würstel can ease my pain?" Etta felt she was in front of a strength of character bigger than anything she had ever imagined.

Following Dora's lead, she started to beg the dog, wishing she'd allowed the waiter to warm up the würstel. She would at least have had something to eat, instead of this cold, wishy-washy thing in her hand.

Then a thought struck her. "I'm thinking about eating! I must be less sensitive than the dog."

BY THE TIME THEY REACHED HOME, THE TWO FRIENDS WERE BOTH exhausted. They collapsed on the sofa, feet up. Leon was lying on the floor next to Dora, trying to sleep, but every so often he'd raise his head as if to make sure the woman was still there. Each time, Dora would pat him on the head reassuringly.

"I'm not going anywhere, so get some sleep, little doggy."

"What do you think happened to the Night Watchman?"

"I've no idea. Maybe he encountered some lunatic, perhaps a drunk or a drug addict who wanted to steal the man's money."

"Oh no, the timing was too tight for any kind of altercation to have happened. And there are two more disturbing details…"

Dora looked at her in admiration. Etta's brain was so quick to pick up things.

"It was all about the timing. The Night Watchman took us around the village, then we came back to the Market Square just in time to catch the clock chiming ten o'clock so we could see the figures appear, and then hear the Master Draught's story."

"What's the legend got to do with his death?"

"What I'm trying to say is that the tour, as relaxed and spontaneous as it seemed, was perfectly timed. Anyone from Rothenburg would know exactly when the Night Watchman would be at the Castle Gate, and that he'd be alone for a few minutes, leaving the tourists to look at the details inside the tower."

"Do you think he had arranged to meet his killer?"

"Oh no. The villain knew that he'd be there at that time, but the Night Watchman – no, I don't think he was expecting anything of the kind. And you heard what the sergeant said: the area should have been lit, which would have made things too risky for the killer."

"You believe the killer knew that the light was out?"

"Or maybe he made sure the light was out where the Watchman liked to wait for his tourists. Can't you see?"

"See what?"

"The killer planned it all. Maybe he used stones to smash the light earlier on to make sure nobody would see him and the Night Watchman."

"But if it was someone from Rothenburg, wouldn't he ambush the man at a less risky moment? There were almost 30 people following him tonight, so why do it then? Why not, for example, when he went back home?"

"Because then the dog would be with him, and Leon would probably have bitten the killer or given him away," Etta said triumphantly.

"You're right, that could be the reason. So he must have known the Night Watchman liked to hand the dog over to one of the tourists. But, Etta, there's one thing I don't understand."

"What's that?"

"Do you think it was safe for a man leading tourist tours to take along a real weapon? I mean, both children and adults would ask to take pictures with him. What if that blade fell on any of them and hurt them? What if the Night Watchman fell and the blade hit someone? I would have expected the halberd to be a fake."

"Or at least have a blunted blade," Etta cried. "You're absolutely right! So, you see, the murder was carefully planned and constructed. Nothing was left to chance. The killer used a real halberd and likely got rid of the Night Watchman's. At this point, I wonder who hated the man so much that they could coldly calculate how and when he should die."

"Maybe the people of Rothenburg already have an idea."

"Yes, if this had happened back home, our fellow villagers would soon be gossiping about who had an interest in killing whom. We will ask our neighbours tomorrow."

"Sounds a good plan to me," said Dora, yawning and stretching her arms over her head. "But just now, all I need is a good night's sleep."

"Shall we put the dog in the basement for the night?" Etta asked.

Dora rose from the sofa, looking at her friend upside down with outraged contempt. She then stood upright, shrugged her shoulders and spoke to Leon.

"Let's go to bed, little doggy. Come with Mummy."

Mummy? Oh my goodness, I hope we haven't stumbled into trouble far more serious than a corpse, Etta thought as she contemplated the dog climbing the stairs behind Dora, his long brown and black ears sweeping each step as he went.

6

A COLD NOSE

A cold, wet something touched Dora's cheek on the pillow. Still sleepy, she turned on to her other side, and as she did so, the cold, wet something buried itself in her nightgown's collar to nestle into her neck. As she squirmed away, she felt something heavy leaning against her bed and scrabbling over the linen.

Dora turned, startled, only to find herself face to face with a black nose, long, freckled mouth and dark, loving eyes. The dog had half climbed on to the bed with his front paws and was gently stroking his head against her.

"Do you need to go out, Leon?"

The dog let out a velvety bark of approval. Dora got out of bed and planted a smacking kiss on his forehead.

"Did you manage to sleep a little? I hope so." She pulled on her dressing gown quickly and went downstairs, the dog following faithfully. In the garden, Leon did all he had to do, Dora picked up what must not be left in the garden, then Leon moved to the gate and pointed his nose towards the outside world, his face serious and concerned. Only then did Dora notice the police car parked in front of their neighbours' garden. The chief inspector and his sergeant were making their way from the house, so Dora slid between the nearest apple tree and the fence and squatted down. She would not have minded saying hello to the sergeant, but the chief inspector was not someone you'd want to encounter, especially before your breakfast.

Marie and Joseph accompanied the police to the little gate, and as the officers left, Dora heard the couple talking softly.

"Do they really think that Johannes has anything to do with Sebastian's death? Are they mad?"

"They're just considering all hypotheses," Joseph said, trying to soothe his wife. "As soon as they find the real villain, all these silly suspicions about Johannes will fade away."

"What if they don't find the killer?"

"Of course they will. I just wish he had not had that argument with Sebastian."

With that, Joseph led his wife back inside and they closed the door.

While she had been hiding, Leon kept looking quizzically at Dora, patiently waiting for her to let him out. Most humans he'd met stood on two feet, but he had felt from the outset that Dora was a kindred spirit to a dog.

"I promise I'll take you out for a walk wherever you want to go," Dora whispered to him, resuming an erect position, not without her joints making some painful cracks. "But later. It's not proper for a 60-something teacher to wander around in her nightgown. Let's go back in now."

Leon looked at the gate, then at the roundish woman with her tousled hair and plump face.

"Later, Leon, later."

The dog shook his head, then condescended to follow her back into the house.

Etta was already in the kitchen, filling her Moka. There had been no way to convince her: either the Moka pot came with them, or she would not leave home. Dora had made a valiant attempt to tell her that other types of coffee existed, and they were all good in their own way.

"Broth. They all taste like watery broth, even when they call it espresso," Etta had said, and Dora had admitted defeat and added both the Moka pot and two packs of Etta's favourite coffee to the luggage list.

As they sat in the garden, eating their breakfast, Etta ignored Leon, and Leon ignored Etta. Dora told her about the police car and what she had just overheard.

"Police are the same in every country," Etta commented. "They always want the guilty party to be whoever they first suspect. Frankly, I don't believe for a second that Johannes was involved."

"But Johannes said himself that he was angry with the man…"

"Exactly. If you want to do someone in, you don't go around broadcasting how mad you are at them."

"Maybe he killed him in a fit of rage," said Dora with no great conviction, playing devil's advocate to test Etta's theories.

"That's exactly what we rejected yesterday. The murder, both the weapon and the scene, had been carefully planned. By the way, did you say the dog wanted to go for a walk?"

Dora looked at her in gratitude. "Maybe he has a favourite park he wants to go to."

"Has he eaten anything this morning?" Etta enquired.

"No, he refused. I even tried to bribe him with some of the meat we bought yesterday for the goulash."

Etta was horrified at the idea that the butcher's best meat could be sacrificed to the hairy thing, but on this point, she knew better than to provoke Dora.

"Maybe he's used to dry food – dog food, I mean."

"I'll get some today, but it's strange he should refuse meat."

ONCE OUT IN THE STREETS, LEON HAD NO DOUBT WHERE HE WANTED to go. The two women passed quickly through the Market Square, dragged along by their eager four-legged companion, then turned right, passing through the belly of yet another tower into a tiny lane flanked by the three- and four-storey timbered houses typical of Rothenburg. Geranium pots sat on windowsills decorated with garlands or wooden fairies and gnomes, and ivy cascaded over every surface.

Leon stopped at the smallest of the buildings in front of a wooden door, its red paint peeling. The building's façade was only wide enough to accommodate a door at ground level and a single window on each of the two upper floors of its crooked three storeys. The window on the top floor had no flowers on the sill.

Leon barked, and a woman opened the leaded window just above them

"Leon, is that you?"

The dog wagged his tail in recognition, but without much enthusiasm.

"You know the dog?" Dora asked.

"Of course, both him and his despicable master. He lived on the second floor."

"That's why the dog has brought us all the way here." Etta pretended to be surprised.

"I don't know why he went to all the trouble to get back here. That man was troublesome and mean. Leon will no doubt have a better life if he's staying with you, but dogs are creatures of habit. Maybe he loved his master, despite all the abuse."

"Was the man abusing the dog?" Dora repeated in shock.

"The man was a troublemaker. He made everybody's life unhappy, and that of course included his dog."

"But would somebody wish him dead?" Etta stepped in, taking charge of the conversation.

"Somebody? You're kidding me," the woman said with a humourless grin. "Half the village wanted him out of the way."

"We went on the Night Watchman's tour last night. He didn't seem that bad."

"Of course he didn't. He wanted to get money from you so he put on his best face. You should speak to the people who really knew him, not the tourists."

"Is there anybody in his flat right now?"

"No, he lived alone and the police have cordoned it off. I hope they will not let his food and waste go rotten and putrefy. It's warm enough without having bad smells all around. I was afraid the dog had been shut in – I wouldn't be surprised if the man caused as many problems in death as he did alive."

"We will decide what to do with the dog. Did Sauer have any friends living nearby?"

"Friends? I'd call them accomplices, partners in crime. Frankly, I wouldn't trust them with the dog. You'd be better off taking him to the animal shelter."

"We'd like to speak to his mates anyway. Where can we find them?"

"Where do you think? In the pub down the road. You need to go out beyond the old walls. But it's closed this early in the day, so you'll need to come back later."

"What's the pub's name?"

"The Devil's Ale. Anyway, I need to go; I've already spoken to the police this morning, and now you. As I said, that guy is still causing trouble, even from hell."

The woman shut the window.

"And that's a fine example of good neighbourhood relations," Etta said. "Our man certainly wasn't loved."

"And poor Leon was mistreated, and he's been so faithful, looking for Sauer and refusing to eat…"

"Must be Stockholm syndrome," Etta cut her short. "I thought that only applied to humans, but maybe I was wrong."

"Leon, dear, we can't just walk in. Your owner is no longer here, please come along," said Dora.

The dog sat on the threshold, his nose still pointing towards the door.

"Come on, deary," Dora repeated, gently pulling the leash.

"You shouldn't beg a dog, just let him know who's the boss," Etta snapped, taking the leash into her hands and pulling. "Let's go," she said firmly. She pulled and pulled with all her strength, but the dog didn't move a millimetre.

"How come he weighs 30kg when standing up, but 300kg when he sits down?" Not one to accept defeat, Etta pulled some more. "Come on, you old mule, come along," she muttered between clenched teeth. But just as all her weight was tilted backwards as if she was taking part in a tug of war, Leon inclined his head, the collar slipped away, and Etta found herself off balance, waving her arms in the air like a baby bird trying to fly.

"You stubborn hairball! Move, I said," Etta hollered, avoiding what had looked to be a certain tumble and recovering her balance. Leon yawned in her face and passed a long pink tongue around his mouth.

"You go ahead, we will follow," said Dora, taking back the leash and putting the collar on Leon. "We could stop at the bakery – I saw one close to Schmiedgasse that looks a nice place. We haven't tasted the *Schneeballen* yet, and we could try their coffee, too."

"And some window shopping would be nice," Etta agreed, albeit resentfully. "With this stubborn hound pulling us all over the place, I haven't had a chance yet to enjoy the town much."

Dora stood in front of Leon. The dog was not too dissimilar to her father, who had been stubborn to the point of unreasonableness if you confronted him, meek as a lamb if you sugar coated your request. Even so, it took her a good ten minutes before Leon finally conceded that his master wasn't at home and he'd better follow the roundish woman, at least until they came across the Night Watchman.

7

SNOWBALLS IN JUNE

E tta entered a café, a gilded pretzel displayed on the
wrought-iron shop sign sticking out from above the door,
and sat at a little wooden table on the black-and-white
chequered floor similar to the one in the kitchen of their house. It
had to be fashionable in Rothenburg. Dark rye bread still hot
from the oven had been laid to cool on wooden grills, the
counter windows displayed a mouth-watering selection of cakes
and pies, but the place of honour was occupied by a tall pyramid
next to the counter made of *Schneeballen* of all sizes and colours.

The fried shortcrust pastries, traditional to Rothenburg, were
shaped as snowballs. Historically, they had been served with
powdered sugar; nowadays, they were dipped into a variety of
ingredients such as white or dark chocolate, nuts, coconut,
cinnamon or marzipan, giving them a whole range of colours
and tastes.

The owner of the café, easily identifiable as she was wearing
a large chef's hat, was speaking to a smartly dressed blond man
with bulging pale-blue eyes. His suit was beige, a white
carnation emerging from its breast pocket, but it was the unusual
bowler hat on his head that demanded attention. Even so, Etta

43

would probably not have noticed him, but for the fact that, despite their rather rapid German, she understood the man and the head chef were speaking of the Night Watchman.

The chef was trying to maintain a nonchalant air, but she was evidently shocked and kept repeating how she could hardly believe the news when she had opened earlier on that morning.

"I told him so many times to be careful who he associated with, but he never listened. He'd only come to ask me for some bread or a pie whenever he ran out of money."

"He was a stubborn fellow," the man said.

"He was always good at landing up in trouble, too." The woman sighed. "Still, to be so brutally killed…"

"I know, I wonder if the police have a list of suspects yet."

"The sergeant was here earlier on, but she wouldn't say a word. Just that it was a nasty business and they didn't think it would have been a tourist."

"That's a pity!" said the man, folding his newspaper in front of him.

The woman looked at him in surprise.

"Come on, Hannah, you know what I mean: if it wasn't a tourist, it has to be someone from Rothenburg."

"Too bad, but it is what it is." The woman called Hannah looked around as if to make sure all the tables were served and the customers happy, but Etta's keen brain realised she also wanted to make sure she could speak freely and that no flapping ears were listening in. Her eyes passed over Etta, dismissing her as a foreign tourist who wouldn't understand enough German to eavesdrop.

"The postman saw the police car at the Pfeiffers' early this morning. And I've heard rumours that Johannes might be involved."

The man had to lay his coffee mug back on the table.

"Johannes Pfeiffer? Are you kidding me?"

"No, that's what I heard." Her attentive eyes had seen a

woman at one of the tables closer to the door raising her head from her dish and glancing all around the room. "Lena, please could you attend to the lady over there?" As a young waitress rushed towards the table, Etta thought how Hannah certainly took great care of her guests, even in a moment of distress such as this one. Once she was satisfied that everyone was happy, Hannah bent slightly over the table so that no one, not even her staff, could read her lips. But Etta could still hear her softly spoken words.

"You know that old argument? Johannes was keen to succeed Sauer and take over the Watchman tours. It seems only the night before Sauer died, they exchanged harsh words in the Weinstube pub. Half the village heard them…"

"I know, I was there."

"Were you? Then you shouldn't be surprised that it ended up as it did."

"Come on! We all squabble and quarrel almost every day, especially at the weekend when we are a little tired after a stressed-out week and tend to drink more than is wise. But that doesn't make us a bunch of heartless murderers."

The woman shrugged, unconvinced. At that moment, a group of Japanese tourists made their way into the café, so Hannah left the man to attend to her new customers, guiding them over to a comfy seat.

The man opened another packet of brown sugar and added it to his coffee. Noticing that Etta was staring at him, he addressed her in English.

"There's never enough sugar to sweeten a sad day like this."

Etta replied in German, "Such awful news. I'm pleased you don't believe Johannes has anything to do with it."

He was startled. "Madam, you speak German! And you know Johannes too? You're not a tourist, then?"

Etta pushed the red glasses she was wearing up her nose and nodded with an air of importance. "I guess we are and we aren't.

We're here – my friend and I, that is – with a home swapping scheme, which allows us to see places from a different perspective."

"Home swapping? I see. That has to work out as quite a cheap way of travelling…"

Etta was grateful that Dora wasn't there. She'd never either praised or defended Dora's home swapping idea when her friend was around, but she was alone now.

"There's much more to it," she replied with offended dignity, "than cheap travel."

"Really?"

"To start with, we have a real house to stay in. We will remain in Rothenburg for a month, not a couple of hours, and even though we had just arrived, yesterday we had dinner with the Pfeiffers, who are our neighbours. Home swapping is really about sharing and having an opportunity to see places as an insider."

"I see," said the man again, removing his bowler hat. "And I apologise for my misunderstanding. I can see now there's much more to it than saving money, and that you certainly have no need to search for cheap holidays."

Etta felt that her dignity had been restored. There was no problem if the man now believed she was a person of privilege on the quest for an authentic experience.

"By the way," said the man, standing up and bowing at her in a somewhat pompous manner that was as affected as his manner of speaking, "I'm Wolfgang Winter, the producer and director for the Rothenburg Theatre company."

Etta smiled at him, feeling a little intimidated at getting to know a man of art and culture. "And I am Concetta Natale Passolina," she stressed her second name Natale, believing it conveyed a certain noble tone. Then she batted her eyelashes before conceding, "Or simply Etta to my friends."

He took her hand and brought it to his lips without actually touching it. *Just like a real gentleman*, Etta thought.

"Would you mind if I sat here for two minutes? Although I see," he indicated the table laid for two, "you're waiting for someone."

"My friend," and she was grateful to use the feminine word for friend in German, leaving no room for doubt. "She should be here soon, but please have a seat in the meantime."

Once he was settled in front of her, Etta decided it was exactly the right time to ask questions.

"I heard you mentioning that you're familiar with the Pfeiffer family…"

"Rothenburg is such a small town, I'm afraid we all know each other."

"Rothenburg is not that small. You see, I live in Castelmezzano in Southern Italy with a population of only 800. That's what I'd call a small village… But no, I digress. I heard you saying you don't believe Johannes could be connected with the murder."

"He's a young guy in love," Winter said sympathetically. "Who hasn't been there once? And no, I don't think he could hurt a fly."

"That's a very good point. Because we are – I mean, my friend and I – convinced of exactly the same thing."

The man looked at her with an expression of surprised amusement, relaxing Etta enough to continue.

"But I also heard you say that the deceased had a tendency to land himself in trouble. What did you mean, exactly?"

"You are a careful listener, I'm glad to hear." Winter took his bowler hat in his hands and turned it around, as if the gesture would help him to find the right words. "You see, Sebastian Sauer used to mix with the wrong people from time to time. It's also true that off-season, he had to augment his income with little jobs, side-hustles here and there. He'd do some repair work on a house, then help out at a restaurant or a tourist attraction getting ready for the holiday season. He also worked for me."

"For you? Really?"

"Yes, he helped me out a few times. Rothenburg doesn't have a proper theatre, so most productions are in the open air, or during the colder months, in buildings we adapt for purpose. Sauer helped with the electrical systems and overall set up, but as we don't have a great deal of actors, he also had walk-on parts in some productions…"

"How would he do his tours if he was appearing in your shows?"

"That was mainly off-season. But no longer than a couple of weeks ago, he didn't turn up for a show in an old mansion house. It was an important event for our company as it was bringing in a little money – so handy when we're just starting the Rothenburg Open Theatre season. At the last moment, I had to stand in for him." He laughed, leaning his temple on his hand. "I was mad at him and sacked him the very next day. But that was exactly the kind of guy he was: unreliable, but not as bad as some locals may portray him. He drove all of us mad, but for different reasons."

"Well, I guess he would have done if you depended on him to do things and he let you down. Did he do these odd jobs you mentioned for anyone in particular?"

"He often worked in the vineyards around Rothenburg, such as the Goldene Traube, if I remember rightly."

Etta made a mental note of the vineyard's name, but didn't let it distract her from the main purpose of the conversation.

"You said something about him mixing with the wrong kind of people. Did you have someone specific in mind?"

"Nothing escapes your notice, I see. I've heard our man was seen a bit too often in a certain pub frequented by some – how can I put it mildly? – unsavoury folk, maybe."

"Are you referring to the Devil's Ale pub?"

The man tilted his head and opened his mouth in surprise.

"Madam! Didn't you say you've only been here for 24 hours?"

"Indeed."

"And you're already familiar with Rothenburg's hidden secrets and dingy places? Frankly, I'm impressed. But anyway, yes, that's the very place." He took a look at his watch and stood up. "I'm so sorry, I'm afraid I have to go, and I haven't told you about our theatre productions yet; you might even want to become one of our generous supporters. But no, you have to watch a play first. We're opening on *Hamlet* tomorrow evening, our first play of the season. Do come – I will drop an invitation in your mail box."

"That's so very nice of you," said Etta, flattered.

At that moment, the door opened and Dora and Leon entered. Dora was looking around to enquire whether the dog was allowed in when Lena, the young waitress, came forward, smiling.

"That's Leon, isn't it?"

The dog raised his ears, puffed out his chest, and let the girl cuddle him.

A smartly dressed woman in her forties came in as Mr Winter approached the door. They had just nodded to each other in greeting and exchanged a few words when a scent reached Leon's nostrils and he suddenly squirmed away from the girl's hugs. Pulling at his leash, he strained towards the door, growling and barking loudly.

The woman, startled, gave a cry and rushed behind Winter, who tried to calm her.

"Dogs who bark do not bite, my dear."

"I've never liked that beast. Never!"

Embarrassed, Dora tried to calm Leon down, but the dog seemed to be beside himself, and she had to turn him to face the wall by Etta before he'd stop. The woman moved to the opposite side of the room, as far away from Etta's table as she could get.

Mr Winter was still standing on the threshold, and a French tourist coming in walked straight into his back. As soon as he'd recovered from the impact, he looked at Etta and addressed her in a firm, grave voice.

"Madam, just to make things clear, the Devil's Ale is not a place you should go to, and *never...*" he stressed the words "...*alone*. Be safe."

He touched the brim of his hat and left.

8

THE CHRISTMAS SHOPPE

D ora finally sat and the young waitress brought their orders over: a huge slice of strawberry cake for Etta and a *schneeball* with almonds and chocolate for Dora, who had gone over to the huge layered pyramid to choose her first ever taste.

"I guess it's the same old story," said Etta, eyeing Dora's pastry. "It won't taste as nice as it looks." She was satisfied with her choice of sponge, whipped cream and plenty of fresh strawberries.

"Well, it reminds me in taste of our traditional sweets like mustaccioli. Maybe it's not as palatable as a sponge; it might be an acquired taste, but I love it. Maybe I'm used to food prepared in the old-fashioned way." The crunchy pastry proved a little difficult to handle, as she couldn't use a knife and fork, but biting the large sphere turned her instantly into a child with a sticky mess smeared across her mouth.

After they were served their drinks in glass jars filled with slices of lemon and mint leaves – refreshing and pleasant for what was shaping up to be a rather hot day – they commented on Leon's strong reaction to the woman who had spoken to Wolfgang Winter, wondering who she could be. Then Etta updated Dora on what she had discovered during her conversation with Mr Winter.

"As soon as possible, we need to pay the Devil's Ale pub a visit, and possibly the Goldene Traube vineyard too.

"Most certainly, dear," replied Dora.

The young waitress brought over a bowl of fresh water and a little treat for Leon, who shook his head. He took a few laps of the water, but refused the food.

"Oh, he's so sad, he's never refused our biscuits before."

"Don't you worry, dear, we'll do our best to cheer him up," said Dora, wondering if she'd ever manage to tempt the dog out of his melancholy mood.

Etta felt a little ashamed at the amount of empty dishes on their table, and when the waitress asked if she could bring them anything more, she hastened to reply in the negative. Meanwhile, Dora took her chance to ask about the cooking lessons that were advertised on a leaflet near the counter.

"Yes, right now we are offering two types of lessons: to learn to make schneeballen or pretzels."

Dora deliberated for a long moment, then decided to sign up for the pretzel class. She asked Etta if she wanted to come along, but her friend replied, horrified, that she'd rather bathe in an ice hole in the middle of winter. Such a statement from a person who would dither in the waters of the Mediterranean for 15–20 minutes in high summer before deciding whether she could bear to take a dip in the 'cold' water clearly meant that Dora would be going to her cookery lesson alone.

Once the waitress had brought over their bill and they had paid, Etta was happy to resume planning for more acceptable activities.

"From what I hear, the Devil's Ale pub is only open in the evening. We have the rest of the morning free, as we should try to speak to our neighbours this afternoon just in case they have news from the police."

"We could visit the Christmas market," cried Dora with her

usual enthusiasm, never forgetting she had tourist duties to fulfil.

"The Christmas market? In June?"

Dora proudly took a Germany travel guide out of her bag and opened it on the Rothenburg pages.

"The Käthe Wohlfahrt Christmas Village is partly a shop and partly a Christmas museum, and the shop is made to look like a traditional German Christmas market."

"I don't really like to think about Christmas before I've had my dose of summer sun and hot weather, but I can put up with this market of yours if you're that keen on it. How about the dog? Should we drop him at home?"

The effect of her words on Leon was immediate. His ears drooped more than ever, sweeping the floor.

"Let's ask if they'll allow him in. After all, it's only a shop."

The dog stood up and wagged his tail with determination, obviously voting for the second proposal.

"Two against one, you've won," grumbled Etta.

Flicking through Dora's tourist guide, Etta found a reference to the Goldene Traube vineyard. Apparently, the owners cultivated rare historical varieties of grape.

"We could visit there tomorrow. Even if we find nothing out about Sauer, it should still be an interesting place."

They reached the main square. A striking old-fashioned red coach with garlands on the side and the roof filled with all kinds of presents told them they had found what they were searching for. The dog was allowed in provided he didn't pee, munch the toys, bark or bite the other guests. Dora swore solemnly that Leon was a really gentle dog, and in the three went.

The shop was like a village. Cute old-fashioned houses, decorated for the festive season, stood all around the main square with a huge glittering Christmas tree in the middle. Dora clasped her hands at least a zillion times at each section of the Christmas market: musical boxes, crystal balls with fairy-tale landscapes, hand-painted nutcrackers, wooden toys, elf figurines, traditional ornaments for Christmas trees – everything was simply gorgeous. Couldn't Etta imagine how beautifully their home would be decorated this year?

Less than a month had passed since the two women, in order to save themselves from the greedy hands of the Italian tax revenue system and survive on their meagre retirement cheques, had decided to share the same house and car, thus saving on expenses. In previous years, Etta's efforts for the Christmas season had amounted to no more than a tatty ready-decorated Christmas tree that stood under a metre tall and a few socks on the mantelpiece for when Maddalena, her daughter, visited for the season with her naturopath husband and their son. But Dora had a passion for taking care of things, and Etta figured their house would end up dressed more finely and shining more brightly than the whole Rothenburg Christmas market. Not that she disliked the idea, she had to admit. But each time Dora went into paroxysms of jubilation at the cutest item she had ever seen – which was pretty much every item in the shop – Etta's eyes went to the price tag and her eyebrows jolted up her forehead almost to her hairline.

"Is this made of gold?" she'd spluttered for at least the fourth time when a shop assistant approached her and asked her if she'd prefer Christmas ornaments handmade by local artists who were rightfully paid for their hours of work or plastic items made in sweat shops where people, many of them children, worked in pitiful conditions.

For once, Etta had no reply.

When they left the shop, a Japanese woman approached them and, indicating a small street on the other side of the square, spoke in the most mechanically syllabised English imaginable.

"Dere's anodder souvenir shoppe, it's from a nice grandmaaa, it comes slightly cheappar."

They thanked her, and then Dora cried, "Maybe it's Johannes's fiancée's shop. He said it was hidden in a little alley."

And once more, Dora was right.

Outside the shop, rather than a romantic vintage coach, a Harley-Davidson with an image painted on its side that looked more like modern graffiti than a Christmas picture took pride of place. The shop, by contrast, was filled with a collection of traditional cuckoo clocks on the walls and displays of wooden toys all around, and a whole room was dedicated to Christmas items.

An old woman with short white hair, a bandana around her neck and an expressive face came forward to greet them. Her voice cheerful and pleasant, she asked them if it was their first time in Rothenburg and if they liked her small town. She mentioned that she loved riding her motorbike along the road through the surrounding vineyards, even though her family had tried all sorts of ways to dissuade her.

"Why would they do that?" Dora asked.

"Well, they say that once one is ninety, the most exciting thing one is supposed to do is watch a soap opera on TV and crochet."

"Ninety?" asked Etta in surprise. She had thought the woman, with her erect figure and peachy skin, was in her seventies.

"Well, I've just turned 86, but to my relatives, that's near enough to 90."

"My daughter thought I was ready for the scrap heap as soon as I turned 50," Etta said sympathetically.

The woman looked out of one of the windows that gave on to the road. A young woman was coming in.

"This is my granddaughter. She will keep this shop going when I am no longer here. Charlotte, we have two ladies here from Southern Italy."

Charlotte had light brown hair, a thick fringe that couldn't hide her shining blue eyes, a slim figure and an enchanting air about her. She looked at them, noticing Leon.

"You're not the guests at Dieter and Clara's home, are you?"

"Indeed, that's us."

"I am so sorry I couldn't make it for dinner last night, but I was at the theatre for our rehearsal. But Johannes has taken an instant liking to you…" Then she stopped abruptly.

It's as if she fears, thought Etta, *that she shouldn't be trying to pass her boyfriend off as a pleasant person when a rather grave accusation has landed upon his head.*

Clearly Dora felt the same. She took Charlotte's hands in hers.

"Don't you worry, dear, we think Johannes is a splendid person. He told us about this shop of yours and we decided to have a look. In fact, I'd love to get a few early ideas for Christmas."

Charlotte flashed her a smile full of gratitude.

"Don't you like cuckoo clocks?" her gran asked Dora.

Etta was horrified. Cuckoo clocks were fine in a mountain hut of some sort, but would look ridiculous in a house in Southern Italy. Luckily, for once Dora wasn't carried away by one of her enthusiastic spells.

"They are lovely indeed, but we already have an ancient pendulum clock in our living room, a very nice piece that has been in Etta's family for generations. The two would neither look nor sound good in the same room, I'm afraid."

"That's a real pity," said the old woman, "as nothing can make the passage of time seem as precious and full of surprises as a cuckoo clock. But I see your point." Seeing a group of Chinese tourists entering the shop, she added, "Charlotte, I'll deal with these customers. You accompany our guests to the Christmas room."

Nutcrackers in all sizes and shapes, nativity scenes carved in wood with small lights on the comet star, musical boxes with bright green wooden Christmas trees and a collection of Santa Klauses awaited them. Dora chose some painted wooden decorations for the Christmas tree: two smiley angels, a chubby bright red Santa, a reindeer whose legs you could pull up and down using a small pendant along his belly, and some beautiful patchwork Christmas balls.

"Wouldn't it be lovely to have our Christmas tree decorated entirely with items from all the places we visit?" Dora asked Etta with dreamy eyes. Etta pretended not to hear.

"Are you planning lots of travels, then?" asked Charlotte, enchanted at the prospect.

"Just yesterday we received a proposal from Mecklenburg. We hope to have many more in the near future."

Etta sent Dora a pointed look.

"That is if we're happy with this one," Dora amended her words. "Rothenburg ob der Tauber is our first ever home swap."

"Oh!" Charlotte said, sympathetically. "What a shame you end up almost involved in a murder on your very first journey! Rothenburg is such a happy, safe place, I can barely believe this has happened."

"You're absolutely right, dear," said Dora.

"On the other hand," Etta interrupted the conversation before it became too sugary, "we heard there are quite a few people who held a grudge against Mr Sauer."

"He was not the most pleasant of men. He could be rather harsh at times, but killing is such an extreme, inexplicable response. It seems far too excessive, if you see what I mean."

"I guess in the killer's eyes it was unavoidable," Etta replied pragmatically.

"Maybe some sort of discussion got too heated. At times men don't know when to stop."

"But Mr Sauer was guiding a group of tourists. There was no time for a conversation to start, let alone get heated…"

"Maybe it was a stupid joke, or supposed to be a threatening message that went wrong. A sort of accident."

Etta shook her head gravely.

As the Chinese visitors had reached the Christmas room, Charlotte signalled to the two Italian women to come over to the counter in another part of the shop.

"It was no accident," Etta stated. "It was a well-executed plan, everything working to the clock."

Charlotte went pale. Her hands, which were holding the wicker basket where Dora had been putting her stuff, were visibly trembling.

"Did the police tell you this?"

"Who, the chief?" Etta shook her head defiantly. "No, he wouldn't say a word to us. But it was self-evident!" And she told Charlotte about the perfect timing of the execution when the tour group was in the tunnel, taking pictures and having a look at the wooden door; about the only lamp that was not working in the Castle Gardens. Then her eyes fell on a rather disquieting object in wrought iron, displayed almost at ground level next to the counter.

"What the heck is that? How scary!" she cried.

"This is called a shame mask."

"A shame mask?" asked Dora.

Charlotte picked it up. It was shaped like a human head, but larger, and it had an extraordinary feature: a huge, unmistakable pig's nose.

"In the middle ages," the girl explained, "town citizens had to avoid things getting out of hand within their community. If someone's behaviour was, let's say, morally lacking, then a judge would condemn the guilty person to wear a shame mask like this one for a day, or maybe a week, according to the gravity of their actions. All passers-by would recognise both the sinner and the sin, and they'd be allowed to mock and tease the guilty party. Hopefully the public shaming would correct the sinner's..."

"Is this the only shame mask you have?"

"We usually stock a few more. Sometimes tourists like buying them, especially one with a protruding tongue and giant ears, as a souvenir for their mother-in-law..."

Dora laughed, but Etta remained serious.

"I'm pretty sure I saw one of these near the Night Watchman's body. But I don't think he was carrying one around during the tour."

"That's right, he already had the halberd and the lantern,"

Dora reflected, "and a horn around his neck. He had to hand Leon to me as he couldn't hold his leash too. I doubt he'd have been able to carry that shame mask himself."

"It was different to the one you have here," Etta continued. "It looked devilish with a cruel grin and a huge nose with a big lump on it."

"A large nose," Charlotte explained, "stood for someone minding other people's business more than their own."

"If our killer went to all the trouble of carrying a shame mask along to the crime scene, that's yet more proof that the murder was carefully planned and organised."

Charlotte went pale, nervous once more, but Etta didn't give her a break.

"Do you have one of those nosey masks?" she asked.

"I'll check our stores after we close our shop. I'll drop one off at yours, if I find one."

"That'd be nice of you. Is there a library where we could find out more information about these shame masks?" asked Dora.

"Well, yes, there's our library, very close to here along the Klingengasse," and Charlotte indicated the direction through the shop window. "But, if you want to see some actual displays of them, you should go to the Crime Museum. They have a good selection of them and their staff are rather informative."

"Is that a Horror and Torture museum?" cried Dora, who didn't like scary things at all. *Mrs Muir and the Ghost*, she explained, was as scary a movie as she could endure.

"Not in the creepy sense," replied Charlotte, laughing. "They don't have those multimedia effects and audio of people moaning, but certainly in the middle ages, they had quite a few nasty tricks up their sleeves to convince people to spill the beans. As for the selection of shame masks… well, I find that quite innocuous. Funny, even. There's also a painting of a pillory with a man in it, his feet exposed and passed through salt so that the goats would tickle his soles…"

"I think I could bear that," said Dora, a little relieved.

~

DORA AND ETTA DECIDED TO HAVE THEIR LUNCH BACK HOME. AFTER all, living in a house meant they could save some money by cooking their own meals. Checking their letterbox, they found a copy of the *Rothenburg Gazette*.

"Now it feels like we're real Rothenburg citizens," said Dora, giggling.

Etta knew why her friend kept alluding to the merits of home swapping. And although she wouldn't yet acknowledge it, she had started to love their old-fashioned house and the way they were passing the days. In the early afternoon, the garden looked so inviting with its freshness, the Linden flowers' soothing smell, the sunbeds so comfortable, tempting them to pretend to read while dozing off. But as for the Pfeiffer family, they were staying out of sight, as if knowing two pairs of eyes were eagerly waiting for them to appear.

Later, while they were busy watering the plants in the garden and the geraniums on the windowsills with Dora trying to explain the different needs of each plant to a reluctant student, Etta looked at her watch and made her best effort at planning.

"I think we'll leave the Crime Museum for tomorrow morning. Today, we're doomed to visit the Devil's Ale pub which, from what I've heard, sounds more scary than any crime."

9
_____

THE DEVIL'S ALE PUB

The clock in the main square chimed the time as Etta and Dora took one of the tight alleys from there to the city walls. They passed under a watchtower and were finally out in the modern part of Rothenburg. In this area, asphalt and concrete had taken over from cobblestones. The large avenue ahead of them was deserted, but beyond a car park and a construction site, a narrow alley led into darkness. From its depths came a dreadful din – you could hardly call music – filling the night air.

Leon sighed, but carried on walking towards the sounds as if he was familiar with the place. He stopped in front of a purplish neon sign, a few motorbikes parked on the pavement, and Dora raised her brows, silently asking Etta if she was really determined to walk into the building.

Etta had some doubts herself, especially when a bald man as large as a two-door wardrobe came out. Despite the cool night air, he was wearing a leather jacket without sleeves, showing his tattooed biceps, each looked as if a watermelon had been sewn beneath it. He had just a few centimetres of what one would normally call a neck, were it not so thick and so short, and on its left side, two swords were painted in red, their tips reaching the man's ear.

Leon pulled energetically towards the man, who raised a big hand, went down on his knees and spoke to the dog.

"Le… le… Leon, is tha… tha… that you?"

The dog licked his face lavishly as the man stroked his long body and scratched his ears with unexpected gentleness.

"Do you know Leon?" Dora said, unleashing the dog. Whoever the hound trusted instantly became her best friend.

"Of… of… of course." The man's sturdy face contorted into something as close as it could get to a smile. "O… O… Otto and Leon are goo… goo… good friends."

Leon gave a last wiggle, then turned his back on the man as if he knew he was here for business. Before Dora could put him back on the leash, he'd pushed the door open with his mouth and sneaked into a dense atmosphere of stale air, too much alcohol and unwashed bodies. It was more like a room full of bison than men.

As Etta's eyes got used to the darkness enough to discern shapes and faces within, she realised the man outside had possibly been the most reassuring looking among the patrons of the Devil's Ale. She tapped on Dora's shoulder and spoke to her, counting on her friend's ability to read her lips rather than actually hear her.

"I don't think we should go any further in. Actually, I think we'd better leave."

Dora shrugged, and her lips gave the answer Etta had feared.

"We need to find Leon!"

Etta had no time to suggest waiting for him outside, or even better, at home. Dora had already turned her back on her and graciously knocked on one of the bison's backs, asking him to make room for her to pass by. The bison burped, then spread his muscular arms and took half a step back.

"Off you go, madam," he said, grinning.

Dora snaked through a temporary tunnel in the herd and Etta just managed to follow, smiling whenever someone caught her eye. She finally caught up with her friend, who was talking to another huge man with a patch over one eye and tattoos criss-crossing his bald head. From the way she was moving her hands, demonstrating something low and long on the floor, she was clearly asking him if he had seen the Basset Hound. The man indicated straight on along a dingy corridor.

The room at the end of this passage was just as ill lit as the rest of the pub, but much less crowded and the music was not as loud. Here it was actually possible to speak and have some hope of being heard. At a few tables, people were sitting playing cards, their faces serious, the occasional blasphemous curse escaping their mouths. The same menacing combination of bald heads, ghastly tattoos, leather clothing and huge biceps was as much in evidence here as in the main room of the pub.

Leon was winding between the tables, sniffing the floor as if on the hunt. Then he stopped at one of the tables, sat down and barked at the most fierce looking man Etta had seen so far. The huge man played his hand with an economy of movement, as if his mountain of muscles would be better off preserving its energy for some later action. Then, without moving his back or his head, only his carbon black irises in the bloodshot whites of his eyes, he looked at the dog. Leon, indifferent to whoever he was talking to, gave another series of three velvety barks.

"Woof, woof, WOOF!" He was obviously asking a question.

The man drew his cards together and placed them face down on the table. The other three players did the same in a tacit display of obedience and respect. This time he turned with his whole body, and Etta wondered if they were about to be invited for a dinner of dog meatballs.

"Sorry, mate," the man said gravely. "Your master is no longer here."

The dog's ears drooped and his head sagged in an expression of hopelessness.

"Oh, poor Leon," Dora said, going to hug him.

"Are you taking care of the dog?" the man asked.

"Yes, we are," Dora said.

"Only temporarily," Etta added.

"There's nothing temporary when you take on a dog!"

Etta, for once in her life, felt like she could melt into the floor at that very moment.

"I mean," she tried to justify herself, "we do not know if he has family. Maybe some friends or relatives he already knows. We're just tourists passing through."

"Sebastian Sauer had neither family nor friends."

"We were told we'd find his friends here."

"Sauer has never been a brother of the Rothenburg Barbarossa."

"But he obviously used to come here, the dog seems to know every one of you."

"This is a public place, anybody can walk in."

"Didn't you mention some kind of brotherhood?"

"We're a boxers' circle. I'm not sure whether you ever saw Sebastian, but I can grant you he was not one of us."

The people around roared loudly with laughter. Etta thought about the thin and hollow figure of the Night Watchman and could easily understand the reason for such hilarity. Nonetheless, she was too touchy to allow being laughed at, even by a boxers' circle, to pass unchallenged.

"I don't think you've got much to laugh about. The police will be here soon, investigating your relationship with the man."

It was as if a power switch had been turned off. The laughter died away abruptly, glasses and cards landed on the table, murmurs stopped. Seconds later, even the music from the bar was turned off. But, on the plus side, all eyes were now on Etta. She had their full attention, even if it was suspended in the middle of an icy stillness and total silence.

Then a deep, low roar like the inner movement of a volcano's belly before a terrible eruption reached her ears.

"Did you dare mention the coppers?" the man growled. Etta wondered if it was really he who had spoken, so still had been his lips. "You will all walk out and leave this woman to me," he roared: the volcano had erupted.

I'm done for! And I never wanted to join this home swapping folly in the first place, thought Etta, always ready to lay the blame on anything but her pesky tongue.

"The poor old hag," one bison said, rising from his chair.

"Nothing will be left of her," another murmured, leaving the room.

"One more cadaver in Rothenburg," yet another added, his eyes malicious.

A few more murmurs that Etta couldn't catch, then eerie silence as the bison pack exited the room.

The volcano stared at Dora.

"You too, and the dog. Get lost."

"Of course not! Etta's my friend."

At least someone will take care of my bag of bones at the end of it all, thought Etta grimly.

The man was still sitting at the table. He gestured idly at two empty chairs the players had left.

"You sit there."

Gulping, Etta took her seat. Dora did the same.

"So, what can you tell us about Leon's master?" she asked firmly as if she were still a teacher in front of her class.

"What do you want to know?"

"Why did he come here?"

"To drink, of course!"

Dora was using a basic trick any teacher would recognise: accumulate obvious answers, and then ask your student to explain it all with a final direct question.

"There are other pubs in Rothenburg, but everyone in town is pointing to the Devil's Ale as his absolute favourite. And as you say, he was not a member of your gang, so had you some other business with him?"

The forehead of the volcano was beaded with sweat. He

squirmed uneasily on his chair, just like many schoolchildren had done before him.

"Well, in fact, he was in touch with some suppliers in Slovakia, and he would provide us with spare parts for our bikes at discounted prices. But…"

"But?" More than a question mark, Dora's monosyllable was punctuated by a demand for answers.

"But the last time, most of the pieces were in pretty bad condition. Some did not work or were poor imitations that had nothing to do with authentic Harleys…"

"Had you already paid for them?"

"Yes, Sauer wanted his money well in advance, and he refused to acknowledge any fault with the merchandise he sold us last time."

"And then?"

"Then I told him he'd better refund our money or we'd use him as a punch bag in the gym. He finally promised he'd ask his suppliers to get us new pieces."

"And last night, some of you went to the Castle Gardens, waited for him and planted a halberd in his breast?"

"No! I'd given him a second chance, and the Rothenburg Barbarossa always keep to their word."

"Maybe it was one of your men?"

"None of them would ever disobey me!" His voice was firm again. Maybe he had decided the interrogation was close to an end.

"Do you know if other people besides your gang might have had a reason to be mad at Sebastian Sauer?"

"Most people in Rothenburg had a reason or two to be mad with him. Most times, dealing with Sebastian meant trouble of some sort. If you hired him, he wouldn't turn up; if you ordered something through him, he'd come up with something different to whatever you expected. Think I've given you an idea, haven't I?"

Dora nodded, satisfied. Etta, still recovering from a mortal fright, was now as impatient as when they had left their home to get back as soon as possible.

The man stood up to show them out. As they walked along the corridor, a collective "Wow!" of surprise rose up from the crowd. The two women were alive, after having pronounced the word 'police' to their boss; the world must be coming to an end. And the bison crowd, with their scary faces and melon-sized biceps, parted to let them pass, acknowledging their mysterious power.

10

AN UNFORESEEN CONFESSION

The next morning, the scene of yesterday repeated itself. A cold, wet nose reached under the blanket to nuzzle Dora, and then a familiar velvety bark reminded her there was no time to waste.

She checked her watch: seven o'clock.

"You're more punctual than my alarm clock." Dora smiled at the dog, who was now sitting obediently at the foot of her bed. She had to call him twice to come over for a smacking kiss on his head, a clear sign that Leon liked to be asked more than once before deigning to do whatever she demanded of him.

"Unless I am wrong, you're a tad arrogant?"

But the dog was already at the door, showing her his bum and turning his head to invite her to get downstairs as quickly as possible.

When Dora let him outside, Leon was immediately a guard dog on duty. He had to make sure that the garden was in precisely the condition he had left it the day before, a thorough operation that required time and concentration. A simple look just wouldn't suffice; he was a scrupulous dog who had to smell every single plant, tree, bush and grass blade.

Waiting in her nightgown, Dora noticed there was someone

in the Pfeiffers' garden. The figure was sitting on a swing in a little sunny corner, but she was still… well, almost still. In fact, it looked like she was gulping.

"Good morning," said Dora as softly as she could. Marie turned her red eyes towards Dora in surprise. "Oh, you poor love! What is the matter?"

Marie shrugged. "It's just me being silly."

Dora opened the little gate separating the two gardens and was beside her in an instant.

"It was a long night, I was grateful for the early sunrise in June," the woman said, trying to swallow the wracking sobs that had made her whole body shake moments earlier.

"I believe nights are amplifiers," said Dora. "They can be sweet and full of dreams when we're happy and contented, or turn into our worst nightmare when we're scared and worried."

"That is so true."

"But we shouldn't forget that they project the worst- or the best-case scenario. Generally, real life stands somewhere in between."

Marie looked up at her. "Your words are so comforting, but right now I'm afraid I can only see the worst-case scenario…"

"Do you want to tell me what that is?" Dora asked gently.

"Oh no, I couldn't." Marie's eyes were watery again all of a sudden as her head moved in denial.

"Well, if you keep these troubling ideas locked inside yourself, they have a nasty tendency to grow out of proportion in the darkness of fear. But if you expose them, sometimes they end up looking very silly and limp away in the light of truth."

"The police," the woman whispered. "Last night, they were here again with more questions, and they took Johannes to their headquarters for questioning. And they asked us where he was the night the Watchman was murdered. I repeated that he was in his room at 10.30 when I popped in to wish him goodnight before I went to sleep. But…" she looked up at Dora with imploring eyes "…the truth is he wasn't there!"

Dora's head kicked back as if she'd received a heavy blow under her nose. When she'd invited Marie to speak, this hadn't been the outcome she'd had in mind. The police must have arrived when she and Etta were on their way to the Devil's Ale pub, as they had not seen them.

"And have you told the police that?" she asked.

"Of course not. They're all over him, like a spider waiting for the insect to fly into its web. They think they know how things panned out and they're trying to put us under pressure so that we 'confess'. But they've got it all wrong – Johannes would never hurt a living being."

"But maybe by not telling the truth, you're not helping your son. If they discover, or worse still if they already know he wasn't at home at that time, this lie might convince them even more that he's guilty, that you were just trying to protect him from an uncomfortable truth."

"I hadn't thought of that. That lie came so naturally when the chief accused my son yesterday morning. I can't go back on my words now."

"What does Joseph say?"

"Oh, he doesn't know it was a lie, I haven't told him yet. He's such a good-hearted man, he could never tell a lie, so he believes what I said. He trusts me, he trusts Johannes…"

A voice called her from the kitchen window.

"Darling, the coffee is ready…"

Marie wiped away what was left of her tears, patted her face with a handkerchief and forced a smile on to her face. It looked more like a grimace.

"I'd better go now. You won't tell anyone, will you?"

Dora was silent for a moment.

"Please," Marie begged. "I know I shouldn't have tried to unburden myself by sharing such a dark secret with you. But you're so easy to talk to. Please, promise me you will keep it secret."

"I promise," said Dora reluctantly. "But remember that the truth has a tendency to come to light."

"I wish it were so, because then the truth about the murder would come to light. But so many murderers get away with their crimes."

Marie left and Dora returned to her garden and its pretty roses now in full bloom. But even Leon could see how worried she was.

WHILE TAKING BREAKFAST IN THE GARDEN, ETTA NOTICED THAT Dora was unusually quiet and distant. She had even forgotten to serve breakfast to the dog, who since the previous night had started to nibble at his food.

"I thought you'd be relieved that Leon is eating again…"

"Oh, but of course! I'm so happy about that."

"Then what are you not so happy about?" Etta gave a satisfied look around. She loved the patio, the garden stretching out beneath it; she had even started watering the plants, according to Dora's instructions. But Dora was so immersed in her thoughts, she didn't even bother to answer.

I wonder what's wrong with her, Etta thought, and when their silent breakfast was over, she tried to tempt her friend out of her strange mood.

"We should go to the butcher and bakery for some fresh food. Our hosts left us a list of their favourite shops in town."

"Oh yes, of course."

"And after that, I think we should go and visit the museum."

"What museum?"

"The Crime Museum, to see the shame masks. Don't you remember?"

"Oh yes, of course."

"You could at least try to vary your answers! How are the Pfeiffers, do you know?"

"Marie was out in the garden earlier," Dora said, squirming on her chair as if it was red hot. "She seems to be fine, just worried about Johannes."

"Tonight we're going to the theatre," announced Etta, pointing to the letter she had just found in their postbox, containing two tickets for *Hamlet* that evening at the Rothenburg Open Theatre and a polite note from Mr Winter saying how pleased he'd be to have them in the audience. Dora just nodded, as if at home in Castelmezzano they went to the theatre every week. Castelmezzano has no theatre, by the way.

"I met Joseph," added Etta, "when I checked the post and he mentioned we could all walk together tonight. They're a nice family, the Pfeiffers, nowhere near as bad as I was fearing."

No giggling; no explosion of enthusiasm about the family; no defending the home swapping thing.

"I think," said Etta relentlessly, determined to get a reaction from her companion, "it'd be nice to invite them for dinner one evening. That is if you feel like cooking something. Otherwise we can buy some takeaway pizza."

"That's a good idea." Finally, Dora had said something other than 'Oh yes, of course'. Dora placed a bowl of milk, yogurt and oatmeal down for the hound, who came over after she'd asked him three times, smelled the food on offer four times, then started lapping with a studied slowness. She looked at him with gratitude, and then winked at Etta, as if to say, "Look, he's eating!" Afraid the dog might catch on to her relief, she went on speaking with a certain indifference. "I saw in the Baumanns' home swapper welcome folder that they mention a good pizza place, we can ask them if they do takeaways too."

My goodness, Etta thought, *Dora passing up on a chance of cooking? That's so weird, I wonder what has happened to her.* But her lips articulated something different.

"Then let's get moving. I guess the dog will want a walk in the park this morning if we're planning to leave him at home later when we visit the museum."

Before she could realise what was happening, Etta was coming to terms with the fact that if you own a dog, even just temporarily, you have to compromise when planning your daily activities, not to mention your life. But at this moment, she was too busy thinking of Dora to see that.

In her strange mood, Dora was less inclined to notice the picturesque buildings, the cute beamed houses, the flowery corners during their walk. But once they were on the Schmiedgasse, she turned back to look at the Plönlein, so stunning in the golden morning light and empty at this time of day. There were no avalanches of tourists who would be unrelentingly swarming the town streets from midday to evening, turning Rothenburg into a busy anthill. Dora couldn't help clasping her hands and, as she had done the day they arrived, she stopped dead in contemplation, then closed her eyes.

"Isn't it internalised yet?" enquired Etta. "Or are you taking extra back-ups?"

"If I do it every day, it will become part of me. I will never think of Rothenburg without thinking we had the privilege of passing by here every day. It's like the little prince taming the fox by love and repetition."

There were times like this when Etta felt she really lacked her friend's sensitivity. Maybe she wasn't a good human being; had she given away an important part of herself in order to march on through the challenges of life? Hogwash! They were investigating a murder. Because believe it or not, Rothenburg, this cutest of towns, had its dark secrets.

11

ROTHENBURG CRIME MUSEUM

D ora and Etta arrived at the red Church of Saint John. Its
ground floor featured tall, picturesque arched Gothic
windows, while the steep four-storey roof, which had once
worked as a granary, looked somewhat disconnected from its
spiritual lower part. From the Saint John's Well, just in front of
the church, and the Aquarius Fountain, they made their way into
another cobbled alley with a wall on one side and a succession of
pretty buildings ahead.

They stopped in front of the Renaissance building on their
left. The Crime Museum invited them in through the
umpteenth arch and porch they had seen since their arrival two
days earlier. Etta was irritated as Dora had refused to leave
Leon back home. She was insisting they could either take it in
turns to visit the museum or ask if the dog would be
allowed in.

"They will laugh in our faces!" Etta had protested.

"It won't do any harm to ask, and if they laugh, good for
them. It will make them healthier people."

The problem with dog owners, thought Etta, *is that, like cigarette
smokers, they refuse to acknowledge how tiring their behaviour is to the
rest of humanity.*

"You go in and ask," said Etta, offering to hold the leash only for the time strictly necessary for Dora to complete the task.

When she came back, Dora had a winning smile on her face.

"What a nice young lady! She said we can leave Leon with her while we visit the museum. I've got our tickets."

Etta banged her hand against her head. It was obvious that invasive pet-owners could find partners-in-crime everywhere.

Leon was a bit surprised when the leash was passed into new hands, but the young blonde woman in the museum was pretty and sweet, and she caressed him exactly as he liked, so he agreed to walk next to her and lie behind the counter, provided he could still watch the door from which Dora and Etta had started their visit.

"If he's uneasy, I will call you," the woman said, smiling reassuringly as Dora lingered on the threshold.

At first glance, the museum looked like any other, with galleries of cabinets displaying objects and books, and miniature villages featuring the daily lives of people, an abundance of ancient chairs and all manner of peculiar instruments. It was only on closer inspection that you'd see how thorns and spikes were the upholstery of an otherwise inviting wooden chair, or that the village miniatures showed people locked in stocks and pillories, or wearing shame masks, or imprisoned in a cage for public humiliation. One cabinet showed the sinister cloak of death that had once concealed the real identity of the executioner, though as the job tended to pass from father to son, it was hard to believe citizens of a small town couldn't work out who he was. There was an eye-watering variety of torture instruments – you could only wonder what type of mind had conceived them.

But of all the examples of medieval finesse when it came to cruelty, the exhibit that shocked Dora the most was the miniature of a school, the young pupils being flogged on their bottoms, or sent to face corners behind the blackboard, or genuflecting on hard wooden beams.

"How could they be so cruel to those little dears?"

"The 'little dears' can be true pests, believe me," Etta replied, unmoved. Or at least, not as moved as she had been when she'd faced the grim-looking Iron Maiden, a sarcophagus in the shape of a chubby lady with an enigmatic look on her face that opened to reveal sharp spikes all over the interior. The idea of being shut inside and squeezed in between the spikes was simply petrifying. "Education in those days was imposed upon the children quite brutally, but maybe it was more effective than Maddalena's compliant way of bringing up her rascal."

"How could you say that? Your grandchild is so cute."

"A spoiled brat, you mean."

They silently continued their disturbing visit.

"There they are, finally!" cried Etta. Glass cabinets in the centre of yet another room were filled with displays of wrought-iron shame masks.

They went closer to read the labels next to the displays. As Charlotte had told them, according to the offence they'd committed, the guilty citizen would be condemned to wear the appropriate shame mask for a day or more. One mask had a long tongue to signify the blabbermouth, vine leaves on the ears were for those too inclined to overindulge in alcohol, and a pig-shaped nose punished those who were dirty. There was even a flute shame mask for off-key musicians.

Among the displays, the two friends found the exact mask they had seen at the crime scene. Not only was its nose huge and lumpy, but it featured a snake and a couple of devilish horns on its hairy forehead. The label said the large nose signified a tendency to stick one's own nose into other's people business, while the snake and devil alluded to the bad thoughts the wearer might indulge in.

"Well that explains quite a lot in principle, but tells us very little of the specific reason the Night Watchman was killed," Etta murmured. "I think we can exclude bad thoughts as a motive…"

"Unless we're dealing with some fanatical obsession."

"I'd rather concentrate on the hypothesis that Sebastian Sauer stuck his nose in where he was not supposed to."

"Are you thinking of the Rothenburg Barbarossa?"

"That's one possibility, but as we've heard, he used to do odd jobs here and there. We should really look for more information on where he's worked recently."

The exit was on the other side of the tower by which they had entered, in a nice courtyard of green hedges and trees. Close to the exit was another strange instrument: a cage suspended from a long wooden arm.

"And what's that?" said Dora. "I thought we had finished with the grim stuff."

Etta got closer to the label and read aloud, "This is the baker's seat. If they cheated on the weight of bread, bakers were ducked into cold water to a greater or lesser depth, according to the measure of their fraud. That's genius," she cried enthusiastically. "I wonder why they banned it."

Dora looked at her in shock.

"Don't tell me," said Etta, "you haven't noticed that Stefano back home cheats on the weight of Parmigiano and San Daniele ham."

"I've never noticed."

"I have, and that's despite his shop already being the most expensive delicatessen in town."

Dora shook her head, unconvinced. But then, according to Dora the world was full of philanthropists and no one ever thought badly of their fellow humans.

They walked back to the ticket office to fetch Leon, who wagged his tail in pleasure when he saw them.

"Did he behave well?" Dora asked.

"A real treasure, I will miss him."

"You don't have a museum shop, do you?" asked Etta, looking around.

The young woman chuckled. "Usually it's kids who ask that question…"

"Not old hags like us?"

Leon's new friend blushed. "I didn't mean that."

"No, of course not, just kidding."

"But if you want to see more, we are setting up an open exhibition scattered among the squares and green spaces of Rothenburg," and she handed them a map, drawing a circle with a pencil. "The exhibits in town are already there, but we're still working on the part of the exhibition beyond the walls. They should be ready by the end of next week."

"What if I want a replica of the shame masks?"

"You could ask the souvenir shops if they stock any."

There was the hurried tick, tick, tick of high heels on the stone floor. Quick as a flash, the young woman pushed Leon back under her desk.

"Has the post arrived yet?" a smartly dressed woman demanded.

"Not yet, Mrs Fundstück, but I will ring the office as soon as it does."

The woman nodded and turned away, tick, tick, ticking back in the direction she had come. The girl sighed in relief.

"She doesn't like dogs," she whispered.

"But who is she?" asked Etta. She had recognised the woman as the same person they had seen the day before in the bakery – the one Leon had growled at.

"She's the museum director."

"Really?"

"Really."

"Did the late Mr Sauer ever carry out any odd jobs for you?"

"Oh yes, on more than one occasion. The last time, he was painting one of the vaults after removing mould from the walls."

The clicking heels approached again. This time, the director stopped to look at the two older women. A flicker of her eyes told Etta that she had recognised them, too.

"We met yesterday in the bakery," Etta told her, anticipating her question.

"I remember, is there anything we can do for you?"

"We've just finished our tour of the museum, and this young woman was informing us you have an outdoor exhibition going on."

"Yes indeed, I hope Luisa has provided you with a map."

Etta showed it to her.

"In fact, she was telling us that poor Mr Sauer used to work for your museum too…"

The woman's eyes widened and her face went paler than the white walls. She bent over the counter to confront Luisa, then her attention was distracted.

"What's that funny moving bag beneath your desk?"

"That's Leon… the ladies' dog. I offered to take care of him while they visited the museum…"

"I've told you before, dogs aren't allowed on our premises…"

Etta interrupted. "Yes, we know and we very much appreciate this dog sitting service you offer, meaning the poor beast didn't have to be left all alone in our house. We will certainly leave a five-star review on TripAdvisor."

The 'poor beast' got up, but before he could face the museum director, she nodded, gulped hard as if she was swallowing a frog, barely acknowledged them and returned to where she had come from.

When she had disappeared along the corridor, Luisa could finally speak.

"Thank you so much, madam, you've saved me from a very harsh reprimand."

"And I don't want to think how harsh a punishment can get in a place like this."

Their eyes locked and they burst into quiet laughter.

"You'd better go now, before the hydra comes back," said Luisa, handing Leon's leash to Dora.

"But we wanted to ask you about Mr Sauer…"

"How about tomorrow? It's my day off and I can meet you at

the Reichsküchenmeister Café in front of St Jakob's church for a cup of coffee in the afternoon. Let's say at three?"

"That sounds great," said Etta, satisfied.

"And thanks so much for taking care of Leon," added Dora.

Leon woofed his bye-bye and the trio left.

"ETTA, LEON TOOK AN INSTANT DISLIKE TO THAT MUSEUM DIRECTOR yesterday. Do you think…"

"Yes, I think we finally have a lead. It's a pity we have to wait till tomorrow to know more."

"But he didn't bark at her today."

"Of course not, he hardly saw her, hidden behind the counter as he was."

"That's what I thought too. But why would she wish Sebastian Sauer dead?"

"That we don't know… yet. Let's wait until we've heard what Luisa has to say tomorrow, and then we might find out."

As they were speaking, Leon had led the two women smoothly but decisively along the Burggasse without them realising it, and before long, they found themselves facing the Castle Gate, beyond which the crime had occurred. The dog kept pulling in that direction. Dora was hesitant, and if Etta was honest, she was too, but she didn't like to show it. Instead, she looked Dora straight in the eyes.

"We can't avoid the place for the rest of our stay. Let's get our return over and done with. It is also on the way to the vineyards."

Despite the geraniums that seemed to overflow from every windowsill, despite the cute restaurant tables laid out in blue-and-white chequered cloths with vases of flowers on each one, despite the pastel coloured walls of the beamed houses, the austere tall rectangular shape of the tower and its dark shadow sent shivers through Dora's spine. And Etta was not as indifferent as she pretended. They didn't stop to look at the small wooden door in the passage, as all the other tourists were doing; they didn't search for the mask from which hot oil was poured on invaders; they passed through as quickly as possible. Even the ever-compliant Dora didn't allow Leon to stop in each corner to smell and appreciate what his peers had left on the walls and clumps of grass between the cobbles.

They were on the bridge, its low walls adorned with more vases containing flowers of every possible colour, making a rainbow look modest by comparison. From there, they could see the old moat. Now that the water was long gone, luscious grass, bushes and trees had turned it into a park where laburnums exploded in a frenzy of yellow clouds.

Out of the second gate they went to find themselves immersed in what looked like a cultivated English garden. Mature horse chestnut trees were heavy with their big white blossoms. Turning back towards the town, they gasped at the fairy tale appearance of the Burgtor, its two pinkish towers, with roofs like dollops of whipped cream over their fat bellies, contrasting with the tall, austere watchtower and the stone walls expanding to protect the town. It was hard to believe that just two nights before in these very gardens, a brutal murder had taken place.

Only Leon seemed unmoved by all the beauty. Instead, he pulled to reach the exact spot where his master had been found. Then he looked up at Dora as if asking her why the man was hiding from him.

"Let's move on," Etta said, unable to hold the dog's puzzled expression. "This must be the road to the Toppler Castle, though I don't think we have time for a visit today."

Etta was disappointed to discover a few minutes later that the castle looked more like a tree house, perched as it was on top of a brick base.

"If there's one thing missing in Rothenburg, it's a real castle."

"Ah!" Dora laughed heartily. "It's funny you should say that.

Before we came here, I read a murder mystery by Elizabeth Peters, *Borrower of the Night*. It's set in Rothenburg, and she made up a castle. Drachenstein, she called it."

"Life is easy for silly writers. Whenever they need something, they can just make it up."

Etta replied disapprovingly, but she decided she'd have a look at the book. She had started to love Rothenburg, and she believed reading novels set in specific locations helped you get familiar with new places and discover new things.

By now, they were surrounded by dense forest. Between the thick foliage, they caught glimpses of the city walls, and above rose Rothenburg's spires and taller roofs. As they continued their walk along the Tauber, the darkness of the forest opened up every now and then to the tender green of vine rows.

They stopped in front of a sign indicating that the Goldene Traube vineyard was open to visitors for tasting tours. In the distance, they could see a traditional half-timbered house, the lower part all white, the beams on the higher part of the building red, a pleasant contrast to the greenery surrounding it. Beside it, a large wooden patio looked as inviting a place as any for a well-earned rest.

12

THE GOLDENE TRAUBE VINEYARD

They were lucky. A wine tour was due to start soon, but they had a few minutes to sit down and refresh themselves. As, Etta realised with alarm, was becoming the norm, Leon was the first to be served with a large bowl of water.

Finally sipping their fresh lemonade, the two friends noticed a young woman balancing on vertiginous stilettos. Picking up some folders and papers from next to the counter, she had a certain aloof air about her. She was undoubtedly the only woman there who had bothered to dress up.

Talking to her was a man in his sixties. His face was smooth and beardless, his cheeks slightly red, and his bluey-grey eyes were hidden behind a pair of small-lensed glasses. The woman's shrill voice was asking him about the theatre sponsorship for the current year, and as he handed her an invoice, she placed it on top of the pile she already held and walked off, slinking between the admiring stares of most men present.

When the waitress came by to pick up their empty glasses, Etta couldn't help enquiring about her.

"Oh, I know who you mean. That's Mrs Schilling, she's the owner's bookkeeper. She wouldn't ever go unnoticed, would she?"

"She'd go unnoticed in Frankfurt, I guess," Etta replied. "Not on a vineyard. I must say, she managed those stilts well on this tough terrain."

The waitress didn't share Etta's admiration and rolled her eyes.

"I can't stand her. Anyway, the boss is about to start the tour if you'd like to join him."

The man who had been talking to Mrs Schilling introduced himself as Franz Fass, the owner of the vineyard and descendant of a family that had been in the winemaking business for five generations. He would be accompanying them around the property to see the different vineyards, and then the cellar where they could taste three of the Goldene Traube's speciality wines.

The tour was in English for the benefit of a bunch of enthusiastic American tourists. Franz's English was heavily accented, but his good nature, the way he'd cry "Ach!" every time he couldn't come up with the right word, and the stories he had to tell enthralled his audience.

The view of the vineyards stretched down to the banks of the Tauber, running between a picturesque overhang of willow trees, and all the way up to the Rothenburg walls, surrounded by the dark green forest they had come through. On the other side of the property, they could see the orchards of apple and cherry trees, and fields of corn.

"We don't have a large property, only six hectares of vineyards, which is good to avoid the spread of disease. The natural barrier of other plants and trees also helps. Besides which, you should really try our cherries. You are lucky you're visiting in June."

Both Etta and Dora made a mental note to buy some cherries as soon as they returned to the property.

When showing them the old wooden barrels in the cellar, Franz became particularly lyrical, revealing how proud he was of his work.

"There are good things in modernity, but there are also things that should stay traditional. I can assure you there's nothing to beat wooden barrels, unless you're running a large-scale industry. But if you're cultivating grape varieties from historical vineyards, such as the one I've just shown you, then you would do them an injustice by using steel barrels – such a cold, clinical material. Wooden barrels shape and give personality to our wines. They're as much part of the winemaking process as the weather, the mixture of grapes, the local water and the limestone soil."

People clapped their hands with enthusiasm.

As the wines were opened and served, the Franconian Tauber as well as the historic varieties, a man in his twenties entered and Franz introduced him.

"Martin, my son. He is carrying two bottles of a light red wine made from the Tauberschwartz grape – a vine that most people believed had been lost to the more profitable modern ones, until a local expert recognised it in a private garden and called a few keen producers to involve them in an ambitious revival process.

"This is the ideal wine for your romantic dinners," said Franz, winking at Dora. "A waltz playing, a red rose, flickering candlelight…"

Dora flushed while the other guests giggled.

Franz brought the tour to a conclusion. "We're lucky," he said, nodding at his son. "We have the honour of carrying forward 1,200 years of Franconian wine culture, and passing it on to our children."

More applause.

"You can buy your wine in the shop upstairs, and we can also serve you a light lunch on our patio. For all her faults, I must acknowledge that my wife is a good chef!"

"That's exactly what we need," said Dora.

"Yes, please let's get some food or all this wine will go to my head," added Etta.

"For Italians, wine and food go hand in hand," said Franz,

accompanying them to the partially shaded patio. "That's a good habit."

Leon went to sniff him and say hi. The man went down on his knees to pat and rub him in a game Leon seemed to enjoy more than any other.

"And now that the tour is over, I can finally pay this furry friend the attention he is due," Franz said, a slight crack in his voice. "He reminds me of Leon."

"He *is* Leon." Then Dora felt she had to explain. "We were taking Mr Sauer's tour when... it all happened."

"I see, the poor devil..."

"You knew him?" asked Etta, feigning surprise.

"We all did in Rothenburg, and every now and then he helped us out here when we needed to mend fences, and during the harvest. Maybe not the most hardworking person I knew, but despite his questionable manners, he was fun to be around. And Leon accompanied him at all times."

"So you had a good relationship with him?"

The son was busy filling glasses. Etta noticed he spilled a bit of wine as he looked up at her question.

"Good enough. But at times, he could stretch the patience of a saint. He was never on time and he liked to taste the wine a little too much. But once he finally got started on something, he'd do a good job."

"You hadn't had a quarrel? The last time he was here, you parted on good terms?"

Martin had flushed visibly as his father and Etta spoke. Although he was trying to look as if he was otherwise engaged, it was obvious he wasn't listening to a word his customers were saying, leaving questions unanswered.

"We had numerous squabbles, but we always parted on good terms. As I said, it could be hard to get him started on something, but in the end he did a good job and I paid him willingly."

"And when was the last time he was here?"

Franz looked at her keenly. This series of questions, so precise, fired one after the other, wasn't the casual conversation he'd been expecting.

"We painted the white fence and lower floor of the house… ooh, no more than ten days ago. Normally, we try to do maintenance work earlier in the year, but this spring was far too wet. And we need to get ready for the peak season; in July and August, tourists will flock in. Then we have September and October for harvesting and winemaking."

"And did you notice anything unusual about him?"

"Dad," the young man interrupted them curtly, "customers are waiting for your advice on the wine to buy."

"He was just the same impossible Sebastian Sauer as ever," said Franz, bowing as his son sent them an angry look. "Duty calls, pardon me."

Franz's wife served them an exquisite meal of dumplings with a potato and yogurt salad and local sausages. Maybe it was the fact they were eating in the open air, but this time Leon accepted a couple of sausage bites that Dora slid to him under the table whenever Etta was looking elsewhere. Afterwards, they felt full and content, but Franz's wife advised them not to refuse the apple strudel with ice cream and whipped cream. It was served warm, and the cooked apples, cinnamon and nutmeg blended in a heart-warming aroma.

"Delicious," said Etta as her spoon scooped up the last mouthful left in her dish.

"I need to ask her for the recipe," added Dora. "It feels like the first time I've ever eaten a strudel in my whole life."

They waited for all the customers to leave before asking the chef for the recipe.

"I hope it's not a secret," said Dora.

"No, at my age you want to spread the word about cooking and encourage others to make things with their own hands. No secrets for me. Let me go and copy it down for you."

The air was pleasantly warm, a few bees buzzing around.

Dora nudged Etta with her elbow and pointed towards the parking lot.

"Look who's there."

Etta followed her gaze. Franz's son was speaking to a dark-haired man about his own age.

"Do we know him?"

"Yes, he was the waiter in the Devil's Ale pub."

"Really?" Etta had good observational skills as far as places and objects were concerned, but not so much when it came to people's faces.

"I'm positive it's him. And I think I saw him sliding something into Martin's hand."

"Like what?"

"Money, maybe? Something the guy could slide into his trouser pocket easily."

The two men disappeared behind the orchards, marching towards the fields as Franz's wife returned with a handwritten recipe. While Dora read it, making sure she understood all the instructions, Etta enquired about the man they had just seen.

"I think we've seen him before, but I can't place him."

"He's Tony. He works at the Devil's Ale pub, but I don't think it's the kind of place you'd be likely to visit. Maybe you met him in town and just remember his face."

"Maybe," said Etta. "Is he here for a wine tour?"

"Certainly not!" The woman shook her head. Despite her smile, she kept looking in the direction of the fields. "But you never know what these young folks are getting up to." She gave a laugh, but it didn't sound sincere in the slightest.

This woman is worried, thought Etta. *I don't think she approves of her son's friend.*

"Is Detwang far from here?" she asked, changing the subject. The woman visibly relaxed.

"Not at all. In fact, you're almost there. You need to go back to the Tauber and continue to your right. It's just a short walk and totally worth it."

They said their goodbyes to both Franz and his wife, and looked one last time towards the fields, but there was no trace of Martin and his companion.

Dora's eyes sparkled with enthusiasm; she badly wanted to see the small hamlet of Detwang. Even older than the ancient Rothenburg, it contained nothing more than a pretty gothic church and a smattering of houses. They hadn't been walking for long before they spotted the tall clock tower and the red roof of the church, which was surrounded by a stone wall. Within was a grassy graveyard densely populated by ancient tombstones.

Dora clasped her hands together, letting Leon's leash fall to the ground.

"How lovely!" She stood still to take it all in, but Etta did not tease her this time. It really looked as if they'd ended up in an old-fashioned postcard. Into the graveyard they went, walking along a small path among the tombstones with Dora explaining to Leon that this was a *different* type of grass. And after she scolded him at the very moment he started to raise his hind leg, Leon had to come to terms with the fact that all this gloriously shiny green grass couldn't be used to mark his ever expanding kingdom. A shame, but that was how it had to be.

They took it in turns to enter the church, the other waiting outside on a shaded bench with the dog, who was happy to enjoy a quick nap.

Inside, the church was a surprise of cheerful pastel blues for the pews and other wooden elements, delicate reds for the columns and ceiling beams. Walking along the aisle illuminated by Gothic windows, alternately arched and rounded, Dora reached the Crucifixion Altar by Riemenschneider, a renowned German sculptor active in the area during the early Renaissance. Never had Dora thought wood could be such an expressive material. Not only the faces of the carved figures at the foot of the Holy Cross, but the folds of their clothes and the juxtaposition and layering of the men's cloaks and turbans with the women's robes expressed their pain, conveying and amplifying the feeling of desolation.

Dora wobbled back outside, reeling from the emotion. Etta, in the meantime, had been processing all they had seen and she was ready to put her thoughts into words. And they were not about Riemenschneider's work.

"I've been thinking and thinking and thinking. I don't like what we've found out. Sebastian Sauer was a regular at the Devil's Ale pub and the Golden Traube vineyard. Franz's son Martin is friendly with Tony, the waiter at the Devil's Ale. And Martin was evidently not happy with us asking questions about Sauer."

"Do you think the three of them were up to something?"

"Most certainly."

"Like what?"

"I don't really know, but we've seen the kind of people who frequent the pub, so I'm guessing it has nothing to do with the cherry and apple trees."

"Yet, into the fields they went..."

13

A GERMAN HAMLET

That evening, Johannes knocked at Dora and Etta's door, asking them if they were ready to walk together with his family to the theatre.

"I'm sorry if I'm too early," the young man said, flushing shyly and bursting with pride at the same time, "but Charlotte is going to play Ophelia. It's her first time as an actress playing such an important role..."

"Not at all," said Etta. "We are ready. At least, I believe so."

She looked inside where Dora was saying goodbye to Leon. The dog, in sulky response to being left behind, was lying still and lifeless on the floor, his backside towards the door, deaf to entreaties, indifferent to promises of future walks and caresses. He even refused to give his paw to Dora who, broken-hearted, had to follow Etta and Johannes before it got too late.

"Let's hope he doesn't destroy the house in retaliation," said Etta, concerned.

"Certainly not!" Dora protested. "His reaction was one of civil disobedience."

Joseph and Marie were waiting outside, both smartly dressed for the occasion. The evening was warm and there was still light in the summer sky. Johannes rushed into the porch to fetch a beautiful bunch of field flowers, blushing as the others teased him for his romanticism.

To the two Italian women, it came as a surprise that Rothenburg Theatre, which they had tried in vain to locate on their maps, was in fact a courtyard in the open air between the town walls and an old stone building. Only the stage was sheltered, and it had the benefit of a set of stairs leading to a loggia that doubled as a small additional stage area.

"Oh, it's so enchanting," gasped Dora, taking one of the hundred seats available to the public. "Look there," she said to Etta, indicating some banners on either side of the stage, "posters advertising the Goldene Traube. We overheard that woman in stilettos saying they were theatre sponsors."

"So few seats for the public," said Etta. "Now I understand why it's so important for the theatre to get financial support. The ticket sales alone could never pay for the show production."

"Die Goldene Traube," Joseph explained, "has been a generous sponsor, and the Municipality of Rothenburg helps out with funds to keep the theatre tradition alive."

"How come they're playing *Hamlet*? I would have expected a German play."

"They alternate German and foreign plays," Marie said. "After all, art has no boundaries."

Johannes joined them after having been to say hi to his fiancée. "Oh, she's ever so nervous," he said, looking as worried as if he were sharing the same agony.

Marie comforted him. "A little tension will actually help her overcome her shyness."

Then, the main lights went out. Only sidelights on the floor softly highlighted the walls around them. Wolfgang Winter appeared on the stage in front of the closed curtain to thank both the public and the sponsors in a brief speech on the importance of supporting art in every form. Then, as he walked away, the curtain rose and the show started.

To Etta's great annoyance, it was a modern interpretation, in which Hamlet was the son of a rich industrial tycoon, Gertrude was a manager with short skirt, high heels and greedy appetites, and Ophelia was an NGO volunteer trying to guide Hamlet onto the path of humanitarian work. Mr Winter, to her surprise, besides being the art director and producer was also playing Hamlet, and there was at least one other person she recognised in the cast. Hamlet's mother was played by none other than Mrs Schilling, the bookkeeper they had seen at the Goldene Traube. Apart from these surprises, Etta, as she had feared, found the play alienating and dull, and it didn't take long before she dozed off.

It was Dora's elbow that awakened her.

"Oh my goodness!" she cried.

Mr Winter, or rather Hamlet, was holding a gun against his mother, the Queen, telling her how awfully she had behaved and how he could not forgive her. There was tension hovering over the entire audience. As Hamlet cocked his gun, his mother cried and begged him to be reasonable. The look on Hamlet's face showed no sympathy; a cold mask had fallen over him, spurred on by doubt and fears. His look almost fanatical, very slowly he lowered the gun to chest height and, as the public held their collective breath, he fired.

Hamlet's mother fell to the floor. Other actors lifted her enough to show the blood spreading over her clothes. The woman heaved a last shrug, and then her head gave up on all resistance and dropped.

The curtain fell.

After a short interval, the show went on, and Etta found it just as boring as the first part. She dozed off again, hoping Dora would wake her if there was something worth seeing. But in the end, she was awoken by the 100 spectators applauding the actors generously for what had to her mind been a stretched-out tragedy which bore very little resemblance to the original. Most likely, people were only clapping as a sign of gratitude that the show was over, and Etta joined in for exactly that reason.

When the actors had taken their bows, the audience gathered in little groups, commenting on the merits of this interpretation and the strength of the character portrayals. Etta joined Dora and the Pfeiffer family, waiting for 'Ophelia' to come out and greet them. A few minutes had passed before she appeared, as pretty as ever, her brown hair delicately framing her oval Renaissance-style face. She was accompanied by Mr Winter, who was enraptured.

"We have a star!" he said to Johannes and his family. "Wasn't she *magnifique*? What style! What an interpretation! Would you ever guess so much passion was hidden in this apparently fragile lady? You were born to be an actress, my dear."

Charlotte blushed as all of the people around her complimented her. Mr Winter excused himself as the press called him over for some interviews, and Dora's eyes fell on the huge bouquet of red roses the young woman held in her arms. Then she locked eyes with the dismayed Johannes. It was certainly not his bunch of flowers.

More people, both actors and audience members, approached Charlotte and complimented her on her performance, and she simply glowed. Although she was slightly embarrassed, it was her moment of glory. Even Mrs Schilling came to hug and congratulate her.

"And to think you didn't want to join us last autumn," she said.

"I had never really thought acting was for me," Charlotte replied, her cheeks going redder than the roses she was holding.

"Oh come on, I think you're being falsely modest. You know exactly how to have men crawling at your feet. In the end, Mr Winter had almost to get down on his knees and beg you. Well done."

"Believe me, I was sincere. I was… actually, I am still scared at the idea of being on stage and that I might forget it all…"

"I meant it as a compliment," the older woman replied, a certain harshness to her voice.

Johannes had kept quiet so far, but now felt it was time to intervene.

"I don't think Charlotte is the kind of woman you're hinting at."

"Oh my goodness, the offended beau. If I were you, I wouldn't worry about what other women say; I'd rather make sure that no other man was walking in my garden," and she nodded at the flowers Charlotte was holding.

"What do you mean?" Johannes's voice rose and what was left of the audience turned around in surprise. "Speak openly if you've something to say."

"I've got nothing to add, young man," Mrs Schilling replied icily, turning her back on him and disappearing into a group of actors.

"Johannes!" cried Charlotte. "How dare you spoil my evening?"

As they left the theatre, the young couple following at a fair distance as they walked towards the main square, it was obvious a heated discussion was taking place between them. And when Joseph asked the two youngsters if they wanted to join them for a drink in their garden, Charlotte excused herself, saying she was too tired. Johannes said he'd accompany her home, and the two disappeared to the left of the pretty Rathaus.

Marie sighed. "Such a pity they should quarrel now. After all, it was such an important day for Charlotte."

Joseph put his arm around her shoulders. "Are you forgetting we had our fiercest fights before our best moments?"

Marie smiled. "That's true. There's the phase of new love, where you only see perfection, then there's the phase of tension when you dissect everything …"

"And then?"

"Then there's the third phase. More challenging than

perfection and criticism is the moment you realise you have to actively create and build a lifetime of love…"

Joseph kissed her. "I have such a wise wife, and I'm still in love with her after thirty years."

14

IN THE STOCKS

The next morning, Etta complained she hadn't slept a wink and asked Dora to take a short walk with her before breakfast to soothe her nerves. Leon, who had not torn down the house while they were away, but had merely slept, was most pleased. A walk outdoors was never a bad idea to him.

They walked out to the vineyards just below the town walls through the Kobolzell Gate, from there to the Castle Gardens, and then re-entered the town through its northernmost access from which they could see the Klingen Tower and the Gothic St Wolfgang's church.

"Oh, it's nice to see Rothenburg before all the tourists arrive," said Dora, as happy and satisfied with her sightseeing as ever.

"I only wish I could put some order to my thoughts. Even walking doesn't help. As soon as we get back home, I'll write them down."

"That'd be most useful," Dora said approvingly. "Shall we go back via the bakery to buy some bread and something nice for breakfast?"

Etta nodded, but they had evidently taken a wrong turn. They weren't too far from the open theatre in one of Rothenburg's many alleys, close to the town museum. A mother was pulling away her child, who was protesting in what sounded like a British accent.

"Please, Mum, let me have one more look. It's so cool!"

"No, I don't think so. And to think the Tourist Office recommended this for children." The woman saw Etta and Dora, and told them, "If you're looking for the stocks, don't bother. It's a bit rough."

"What's wrong with it?" Etta asked, instantly curious.

"The mannequin is horrific! Not as nice as the ones in the square…"

"That's not true!" the child protested. "It's funny."

"Back to our hotel, young man! We'll stick to visiting churches and the Christmas shop today." The woman pulled her boy into the hotel just in front of them.

Dora and Etta looked at each other briefly while Leon raised his nose in the air, his nostrils flaring. He wasn't simply smelling, he was twitching his lips, and his jaw made an almost imperceptible up and down movement as if he was savouring the air with his mouth. His ears up, his whole body tense, he pulled exactly in the direction the woman and boy had come from.

Fewer than fifty yards ahead, they saw the stocks. The mannequin had its head, arms and legs trapped between an upper and lower wooden board with holes cut to accommodate them. It was wearing black stilettos and it wasn't made of straw like all the other mannequins around town. Despite the fact it was wearing a shame mask with a long tongue hanging from its mouth and pointed ears, both women came to the same conclusion.

"That's not a mannequin, it's a real woman!"

Leon let out a low whine and Etta reluctantly bent down to check the woman's wrist as it emerged from the wooden board.

"I'm no expert, but she looks like she's stone cold dead."

~

WHEN THE POLICE ARRIVED, BOTH THE SERGEANT AND THE CHIEF inspector looked incredulously at the two women.

"Couldn't you be content with crocheting instead of corpse finding as a hobby?" the man asked after he had checked the body. Then he turned to his sergeant. "When the scene of crime team arrive, they will remove the mask and we will be able to identify her. I don't see a bag or anything else that may help us, even though she's smartly dressed."

The sergeant nodded. "It's evening dress. I'm afraid she must have been attacked last night."

"I wonder if we might know who she is…"

"I think we do," said Etta, exchanging glances with Dora. The two police officers looked at them with both surprise and suspicion.

"We think it might be Mrs Schilling, the bookkeeper at the Goldene Traube vineyard. She was at the theatre last night, performing in *Hamlet*, and this dress looks very much like the one she was wearing. And the little I can see of her hair seems to match."

"How did you know her?"

Etta hesitated. "We didn't really. We saw her briefly at the Goldene Traube vineyard yesterday afternoon, speaking to Franz Fass, then we saw her again last night playing the role of Hamlet's mother."

Dora gave a little gulp. The sergeant noticed, but she didn't say anything.

"And," Etta's brain was working furiously, "we think there's something weird going on at the vineyard."

The scene of crime team arrived and the chief inspector told the two women to move away and wait for him. Pictures were taken of the body as it was, which took a while, so some time had passed before the scene of crime officers opened the stocks and lowered the body to the floor. The mask was removed, more photos were taken, then a man kneeled down to examine the body. He asked it to be turned on to the other side and pointed at something on the back of the head.

As the examinations continued, the police officers returned to Etta and Dora.

"Has she been murdered?" asked Dora.

"I'm not at liberty to say," the chief inspector replied bluntly.

"But how else did she die?" Etta insisted.

"That's none of your business…"

"None of our business, rubbish," Etta protested loudly. "Since we arrived in this town, it seems we've been destined to stumble on a dead body every other day. We have a right to know."

"I hope that's a coincidence," snapped the chief inspector. "Tell me, what time did the play finish yesterday?"

"It was around eleven o'clock when we left. The show finished a little earlier, but since most of the audience was local, they stayed on to congratulate the actors."

"And what were you saying about the Goldene Traube?"

Etta explained how they had seen Mrs Schilling there, and the fact the Devil's Ale waiter had been there too.

"The Devil's Ale pub?" The chief inspector almost looked shocked as he glanced at his sergeant. "How do you know about that place?"

Etta explained what had taken them there, what they'd discovered about the Night Watchman, their surprise during their wine tour to see the waiter talking to Martin, Franz Fass's son, and how Martin had not looked pleased when they were asking questions about Mr Sauer.

"I wish we could stop the Rothenburg Barbarossa's dirty dealings once and for all," the chief inspector muttered.

"Are they that bad?" asked Dora.

"They call themselves a sport club. They play at boxing and organise gatherings and rides on their motorbikes. But over the years, we've seen a rise of such gangs. Often they're linked to right-wing extremists, and they're not above dealing in drugs, weapons and prostitution. So far, we've never managed to prove the Barbarossa gang guilty, but you said you've met them. I'm sure you've come to your own conclusions as to what kind of folk they are."

"Well, they weren't that bad with us… ouch!" Dora cried as Etta kicked her leg. The two police officers looked at each other.

"Was anyone from the Goldene Traube at the theatre last night?"

"I didn't see the son, but I certainly spotted Franz and his wife."

"And how long have you been here in Rothenburg?" the sergeant asked.

"Well, this is actually our fourth day in town," said Etta.

"You've certainly got to know quite a few people in a very short time, so you're not simple tourists…"

The scene of crime team called the chief inspector over for a consultation. He turned to the sergeant before he went.

"Take their full statements concerning finding the body and what they witnessed yesterday, then let them go." Then addressing Etta and Dora, he added, "And you two, stop sleuthing! I've a feeling that's what you're playing at. We've got victim number two, and I don't want two Italian tourists added to the list. International cases are a real hassle."

The sergeant raised her eyebrows and looked at him critically. Etta exploded.

"You mean if we were German it would be OK for us to get murdered?"

"Not at all," the man growled, "I just want you to stop snooping around as I don't want any more complications than I already have."

The sergeant asked more questions about what had happened the day before. Dora and Etta by tacit agreement decided not to mention the squabble between Johannes and Mrs Schilling. By the time they were finished, a number of journalists had arrived and the police were finding it tough to keep them from the crime scene. When they saw Etta and Dora leaving, the journalists surged around them, asking questions. Etta decided not to respond, but when one of the journalists recognised her as the tourist who had found the Night Watchman dead and asked her whether she had come to Rothenburg to commit murder, she did tell him bluntly to bugger off.

Dora, on the other hand, always eager to please, responded by telling the journalists they had come to help the Rothenburg Police and that they had already carried out a successful investigation back in their little village in Italy, and how they thought the murder was connected with the theatre performance the night before and some important local institutions. By the time Etta made her way through the crowd of microphones and cameras to pull Dora and Leon away, it was probably a tad too late.

"What are you thinking? We want to keep a low profile, so why did you tell them all that?"

"I couldn't stand the idea they might suspect the two of us. And you will solve the case before the police. It's all so theatrical, but I'm sure you can see through the smoke and mirrors."

"Let's get back home as quickly as we can," Etta said, hiding her smile at the confidence Dora had in her. "We can inform the Pfeiffer family of what has happened. Unfortunately, I think the police will be on to them very soon."

WHEN THEY REACHED HOME, MARIE WAS BUSY WATERING THE plants in her garden. She panicked at the news of Mrs Schilling dead, and Etta guessed her thoughts.

"We didn't tell the police about the little discussion Johannes and Mrs Schilling had after the play. I don't think it has any bearing on the case, but unfortunately there were other people present. I fear they will tell the police when questioned."

"Oh my goodness! Let me call him," Marie said, fetching her

phone. "Johannes, is Charlotte with you in the shop? OK, please drop everything and come over. I've got bad news."

Johannes arrived home about ten minutes later, looking rather anxious.

"Mum, what's happened?"

"There's been a new murder, last night… Mrs Schilling."

"Oh my goodness!" cried Johannes, collapsing onto the chair next to his mother. His face had gone so pale, it didn't require Etta's observational skills to realise he was not only sorry for the woman, he was also concerned about himself.

"Try not to worry," Dora said.

"Do you know anything about the Rothenburg Barbarossa?" asked Etta.

"We all know of them. They're renowned as being bullies, and some people say they deal in drugs, or weapons trafficking from Eastern Europe. But I don't know much else, I'm afraid."

"How about Tony, the waiter at the Devil's Ale?"

Johannes thought for a while. "I can't really place him, it's not the sort of pub I frequent."

"And the Goldene Traube? Anything untoward about the Fass family?"

"Their wines have such a good reputation in the whole country. Franz's work has always been respected, and I don't think I've ever heard anything peculiar about his son Martin, either."

"Still, we saw Miss Schilling there yesterday lunchtime, we saw Franz and his wife at the theatre in the evening, we saw the Devil's Ale waiter at the vineyards… I'm sure there has to be something connecting them all."

"I can speak to my pals and see if they come up with any ideas. Though at the moment, I'm frankly just worried about myself."

"About that little squabble?" Etta asked.

"It's not only that. Mrs Schilling was the bookkeeper in Charlotte's shop for just over a year…"

"And?"

"And we had an argument, and I suggested Charlotte and her grandmother refuse to use her services again. That's why she was sharp with me last night."

"What was this argument about?"

"She suggested they didn't declare their entire revenue to the taxman…"

"Isn't that more an accountant's job?"

"Well, the accountant's work is based on the numbers provided by the bookkeeper. I mean, like everyone else, they want to pay as little tax as possible, but in a legal way. I don't want them to get into trouble."

"Do you think she might have stolen some of their money?"

"Oh no, she wouldn't touch their money. Anyway, I've been keeping a close eye on the shop registers ever since Charlotte asked me to help her and her gran out in my spare time. I just didn't like the way Mrs Schilling insisted on certain things that seemed downright dishonest to me. And she, of course, asked for a percentage of what they were to save in taxes."

"So they stopped using her?"

"I told them I wouldn't like to work with someone I didn't trust. They agreed with me that since we had such different views, it'd be better to part company with her."

"Do you know who her other customers are?"

"Other shops, bakeries, the theatre, the Goldene Traube and the Crime Museum. I'm sure there's more to the list."

"The police are here," whispered Marie, who had been keeping a close eye on the window looking out to the road.

"We'd better sneak out the back and pretend we've been in the garden all along," said Dora.

And so they did, just in time. As they exited through the back door, the police rang the Pfeiffers' front doorbell.

15

FOLLOW THE MONEY

B ack home, the two friends didn't stay long in the garden. The Pfeiffers' living room window was closed as soon as the police entered, and there was no chance to eavesdrop on the interrogation.

"Let's move inside," said Etta. "I need to do some serious thinking with pen and paper."

"And we will keep our window shut, too," Dora added.

While Dora prepared breakfast, Etta started to write down a few notes.

"Sebastian Sauer was killed, and then Mrs Schilling. The two shame masks we found at the crime scenes indicate the murders were committed by the same hand. Would you agree so far?"

"Absolutely," said Dora, toasting the few remnants of bread from the previous day. In their rush to get back home, they hadn't stopped at the bakery as they had intended.

"Now, we want a list of suspects. I'd say the Devil's Ale waiter. It was a place Sauer frequented, and we don't know what felonies go on there. My favourite theory is that the waiter and Martin Fass are up to something together. Trafficking drugs, maybe weapons? Maybe they were into something with the Barbarossa gang and Sauer was a not so welcome member of this organisation, although he had proved useful to them in the past."

"So why kill him?"

"Maybe he wanted out of the organisation. You know how it works with these people."

"No, I don't," said Dora, pouring the Moka coffee into two cups full of milk. "Our caffellatte is ready."

"Well, I do. I saw a documentary on TV – I can't remember the actual name of the gang, but it was all tattooed skulls, knives and cut-off leather jackets, just like our friends in the Devil's Ale. And the programme said it took over a year of trials, with different tests to check both your courage and your loyalty, to get into the gang. But as far as getting out of the gang was concerned, that simply wasn't in the rules and regulations. You'd walk in alive, you'd be carried out dead. If you betrayed the gang, your name, photo, all the info they had on you would be spread to the various associations throughout the world. Whoever happened to cross your path would have the right to do you in."

Dora put down the caffellatte she had meant to drink. "Oh my goodness! That sounds so scary."

"Indeed it is!"

"To think we walked right into their lair only a couple of nights ago." Dora lifted her coffee cup in slightly shaking hands and took a sip. "And I had the nerve to question them! But why would they kill Mrs Schilling too?"

"Maybe she witnessed something going on. Do you remember the shame mask she was given? Long tongue, huge ears. Maybe she threatened to speak out about what she'd seen."

"But what did she see?"

"I don't know yet for certain, but I have my suspicions."

Dora looked at Etta with admiration, her plump face as round as her open lips as she let out a long "Oooh" of surprise.

"She kept the records for the Goldene Traube, so she may have noticed things not adding up. Maybe large amounts of money were coming in – much larger than the business could justify."

"I don't understand. Where would this money be coming from?"

"It's called money laundering. If you have lots of money coming in from criminal activities, you can't put it into your bank account, or under your mattress. But if you're the owner of a legitimate business, you can pretend that the business is earning the money, when in fact it isn't."

"I see. And Mrs Schilling had started to suspect something, and eventually found out the whole truth?"

"Exactly!"

"Oh, the poor woman," said Dora, who couldn't hold harsh feelings towards anyone.

At that moment, Etta's mobile phone beeped: a new message on WhatsApp.

"This must be Maddalena, she's always good at distracting me, no matter how many thousands of kilometres apart we are." But on checking her phone, she realised it was an altogether different source of distraction. "It's Luisa, the girl from the museum, confirming she will meet us at the café near Saint Jakob's Church."

"I'd almost forgotten," confessed Dora.

"So had I," said Etta. "But that brings us on to hypothesis number two."

Dora paused, her knife in the air. She had been spreading butter and elderberry jam on the toasted bread for the two of them, but now she felt the tension rising.

"And what's that?" she asked in a low voice.

"The museum director. The first time we met her, Leon growled at her. Why?"

Dora nodded, completely absorbed in Etta's musings as some jam slipped from the knife into her caffellatte.

"We know Sauer worked for her. And Johannes mentioned that Mrs Schilling worked as a bookkeeper with the museum too, and nothing is easier than embezzling money from a supposedly fine and upstanding institution."

"And you think Sauer knew something was going on?"

"He may have seen or realised something was wrong. Maybe he spoke to the museum director about it, which of course meant he had to die. Then she realised Mrs Schilling was a potential witness too."

"Do you think Mrs Schilling participated in Sebastian Sauer's murder?"

"Not necessarily, but if Mrs Schilling knew that the museum balance was not in order, she may have done her sums and come to the conclusion as to who Mr Sauer's killer was. Maybe she even tried to blackmail the museum director, who was left with two choices: pay up for the rest of her life or do something about it."

"And she would have had easy access to a halberd, as well as the shame masks."

"Exactly!" Etta decided it was time to finish her toasted bread before she carried on. "But there's a third hypothesis…"

"Oh! Is there?"

"Well, it's the one we don't want to be true. But we have to consider all things if we want to solve the crimes, even the most uncomfortable truths we don't want to face…"

"You're not thinking of Johannes, are you?"

"Of course I am. We need to reason like the police if we want to figure out this mystery before they do. We know Johannes was furious at Sauer, and he wanted the man's Night Watchman job. You've seen Charlotte and her gran's souvenir shop – it was basically empty of clients, while the Christmas market was full to capacity. But imagine if it was the Night Watchman's shop, how many people would go there to speak to him, to know more, to buy his souvenirs. And that's beside the guided tour business."

"But he's such a sweet boy," Dora protested.

"That doesn't matter. To you, the meanest of thugs is just a little lively."

Dora shook her head, her salt-and-pepper fringe dancing across her face. "Why would he kill Mrs Schilling?"

"She's worked for him too. Maybe she noticed something wrong – we only have his word for it as to what an honest chap he is. Maybe he's up to his ears in debt, so killing the Night Watchman would give his finances a turn for the better. But Mrs Schilling knew about his financial position, suspected him of the murder and told him she was going to tell the police. After the theatre play, Johannes accompanied Charlotte to her place, then ambushed Mrs Schilling and did her in."

"I really can't see him doing anything of the kind."

"But we know he was out last night at the right time, and possibly in the right place too."

Dora winced slightly. Of course, only she and Marie knew that Johannes had been out when the Night Watchman had died, too. To cover her guilt at keeping this secret from her friend, she asked the first question that came to mind.

"But why use the shame masks? It would have taken him some time to set the scene…"

"Whoever the killer is, he or she is behaving normally in their daily life, but we're dealing with a sadistic, calculating and ruthless person."

"Do you think he's finished killing?"

"The killer will stop when he *or she* feels safe, so we don't have the answer to that."

"What should we do now?"

"More sleuthing. We need to find out how precarious Johannes's financial situation is. How prosperous is the Goldene Traube, and what state are the Crime Museum's finances in?"

"My goodness, I never thought such… such theatrical crimes could be solved by looking at sterile balance sheets."

"Always follow the money!" said Etta, happy that she had once more won her friend's admiration.

"But how are we going to check?"

"I don't know yet. Maybe we could ask the police to help…"

At those words, Dora approached the window and let out a gasp.

"They're taking him away!"

"Who? Johannes?"

"The very same. Poor Joseph and Marie look so miserable."

"There's nothing much we can do for them right now. I suggest we go out for some shopping, have our lunch, and then go to see young Luisa. Maybe she can tell us more."

16

CAFÉS, CAKES AND CONFIDENCES

It was a pleasure to sit in the sun. The Reichsküchenmeister Café terrace, facing the Gothic façade of St Jakob's Church, sat under the partial shade of a number of colourful umbrellas and a few large chestnut trees, and was surrounded by geraniums and shrubs. At three o'clock, the bells chimed and people's chatter was drowned out for a few moments. With an abundance of clocks, towers and churches, every single corner of Rothenburg seemed to resonate with merry dongs.

When Luisa joined them, she bent down to caress Leon, who was lying under the table enjoying the shade and the fresh air. Too tired, or maybe just too precious, to get up, he wagged his tail vigorously and rolled on to his back, his paws scrabbling in the air.

"You spoiled little brat," said Luisa, laughing and scrubbing his tummy.

It was just as difficult as ever to choose which of the many colourful cakes displayed within the café windows to try. And the two older women could hardly believe their eyes when three huge slices were brought to their table.

"I wonder how you manage to stay so slim, living in this

country," said Etta, pointing at the mountain of whipped cream and ice cream served beside her slice of strawberry cake.

"We love sport, a lot." Luisa chuckled. "And we don't like tourists thinking we're stingy with our portions."

"I've noticed you like the dog – have you ever considered owning one?" Etta enquired innocently. Alarmed, Dora dropped her spoon in her dish with a loud clatter.

"I'd love to…"

"As you know, Leon is not our dog; we took him in an emergency, but if there's a Rothenburg family up for adopting him, that would be perfect."

Dora's expression was horrified. Unaware of his future hanging in the balance, Leon kept squirming under the table, hoping for more cuddles and attention, his paws still pedalling in the air.

"Really?" Luisa asked. "It looks like the three of you are a family now…"

"Just a temporary one. Wouldn't you love to take him in? It seems you get along wonderfully well."

"You're right, I'd love to say yes, but in September I'm leaving for Lisbon. I'll be studying there for a year, and there's no way I could take him. And even if I could, I'll be out all day long at lectures, so he'd be alone for long periods of time."

"I see," said Etta, ungraciously. Dora could breathe again.

"But you could try the dog shelter, they are really helpful there."

"The police mentioned that place as well. I guess we'd better pay them a visit soon, the dog seems to be much happier now."

"What a pity you don't want to keep him…"

Again, before Dora could get a word in edgeways, Etta cut Luisa off.

"No, it's impossible. We want to travel for as long as we have the strength to do so; the dog would be a hassle."

The 'hassle' had spread himself all over the floor under their table, his underbelly exposed to the sun, his head still in the shade, totally blissful.

Luisa changed the subject. At least she had noticed the discussion about the dog had been hard on Dora.

"You said you wanted to speak to me about Sebastian Sauer because you're investigating the crime. Or rather, crimes."

"Investigating?" said Etta in surprise. Had they been that obvious?

"Yes, investigating. Such a shame you should witness two murders during your stay, I swear Rothenburg is normally a lovely, peaceful place, almost to the point of boredom."

"Peaceful? That's a hoot!" Etta whispered to herself, thinking about the Devil's Ale pub, the possible money laundering activities going on at the Goldene Traube vineyard, the suspicion that Mrs Schilling had been defrauding the taxman, and all that was just a side dish to two murders.

Then a thought struck her. "How do you know that we're sleuthing?"

"Oh," Luisa answered coolly, "I saw your interview at the second crime scene on the local TV news at one o'clock."

"What interview?" Etta barked.

"Mrs er…?" Luisa looked at Dora.

"Miss Pepe, Dorotea Rosa Pepe, but you can call me Dora."

"Yes, Dora's interview," Luisa confirmed enthusiastically. "She was great! She said she handles this kind of stuff all the time back in Italy, and after dealing with the mafia and camorra, you should find it easy to catch the murderer here in Rothenburg. She sounded so cool, like a battle-scarred private investigator…"

"Those moronic journalists, didn't they cut out anything Dora said?" Etta commented, shaking her head in disapproval. Then she squeezed her face between her palms as if to say what's done is done. Her green eyes sparkled, she tossed back her red hair. It was time to move on. "So yes, you're right, we're investigating, and we need more information. The museum director is not around so you can speak freely."

Luisa looked at the other tables. "Yes, that's why I suggested meeting here. At this time of day, there are only tourists around. So, what is it that you want to know?"

"Let's start with Sebastian Sauer. You said he'd been working for the museum, didn't you?"

"That's correct. He'd done odd jobs for us, cleaning and painting some of the exhibits. He also helped to organise classes for both adults and children."

"How did he get along with the museum director?"

"Mrs Fundstück simply couldn't stand him. They clashed from the very first moment he came in, bringing Leon along with him. As you've seen, she's not fond of dogs, and Sebastian's ways did nothing to help her overcome her prejudices."

"Sebastian's ways?"

"He was never on time, not too accepting of her authority. Mind you, he carried out all the tasks he was given in the end, but he liked to come across as more rebellious than he really was…"

"So you think it was just a personality clash?"

"Yes, I'd say so."

Etta didn't look too happy with this response. She carried on, nonetheless.

"How about Mrs Schilling? I've heard she did some work for the museum, too."

"Yes, she was our bookkeeper…"

"Employed by the museum?"

"No, she's… sorry, she was a freelancer. But she used to come in at least once a month, sometimes twice. Sometimes she'd stay for a while and ask questions of Mrs Fundstück or her assistant. Other times, she would drop by only to collect the receipts and invoices she needed."

"And did they get along well? Mrs Fundstück and Mrs Schilling, I mean."

Luisa gave the question a lot of thought before answering. "Mrs Fundstück is not an easy woman to deal with. She's rather strict and she likes... how should I put it? She likes to exert her authority. I'm more mellow; I don't like to put up a fight, so we get along without any great conflict..."

"But Mrs Schilling?"

"She could be rather headstrong."

"But surely Mrs Schilling had to be courteous. I mean, Mrs Fundstück was her client, after all."

"Yes and no. The museum property is privately owned, and it was the family that owns it who took Mrs Fundstück on as director. It was also the family who hired Mrs Schilling. My feeling is the two just tolerated each other because it wasn't in their power to choose whether to work together, if you see what I mean."

"That explains a few things. Still, I wonder if they openly disagreed on anything."

"Well, there were lots of procedures to follow and things to do for the outdoor exhibition: there were volunteers to coordinate, replicas to construct, extraordinary activities to organise. About a week ago, there was a heated discussion between the two women. Not that Mrs Schilling had anything to do with the exhibition itself, except for keeping track of every single transaction, but something must have happened."

"Something like what?" Etta was devouring Luisa with her eyes, to the point where she had forgotten about the cake in her dish. The young woman felt slightly uneasy under the gaze of those keen eyes, but at the same time, she was proud of being the centre of attention.

"Usually Mrs Fundstück leaves her office door open so that she can see employees coming and going along the corridor. From the ticket office, I could hear their voices getting louder and louder."

"What were they talking about?"

"Really, I couldn't say. I couldn't distinguish the words

themselves, I just heard the loud voices. Luckily it was almost closing time and there were no tourists around."

"Do you think anyone else might have heard them?"

"Well, I'm not sure if Mrs Messner, the lady dealing with bookings and reservations, was there. She has an office along the same corridor..."

"No one else?"

"No."

"Is there any way we could ask this Mrs Messner if she heard anything specific? Can we arrange an appointment with her?"

"She's a strange creature, very elderly. She isn't usually keen to speak to strangers, but I can ask her if you want."

"I'd be grateful."

"And..." Luisa looked doubtful. Etta read her doubt and encouraged her.

"Whatever you remember might help."

"Well, I'm sure Sebastian was passing when they were arguing. Not through the corridor, though; he came up from the vaults and went into the museum. He would have been much closer to Mrs Fundstück's door than I was."

"Are you suggesting he might have overheard what the argument was about?"

"Yes, I believe he would have been in a much better position than I was."

"Goodness!" Dora cried.

"Do you think he heard something he wasn't supposed to?" Luisa asked.

"I don't think the discussion was that important..." Etta took a moment before carrying on, "...or the two women would have kept it more private, at least closing the door. But maybe he knew other things about them and this new bit of information only served to strengthen his claims."

"Well, I'm sure he stopped to listen before moving forward," said Luisa conspiratorially.

When the last crumb of cake had succumbed, the four rose

from the terrace and parted. Luisa promised to do some quiet sleuthing on their behalf, while Etta, Dora and Leon took the path towards the nearby St Jakob's church, which they hadn't yet visited.

"This is getting very complicated," grumbled Etta. "And the fact that you went on TV and spoke about our involvement and our sleuthing abilities isn't reassuring at all."

"I'm so sorry," Dora replied, mortified. "I still don't know what came over me. I saw that huge light, the camera and the microphones, and all of a sudden I felt I had to tell them something interesting."

"Interesting, fiddlesticks," Etta said. "Anyway, I'll go in first. You stay with the dog; I don't think the priests will be as well disposed towards him as Luisa was."

Dora nodded. She knew from experience that dogs were not generally allowed in churches, even back in Italy where statues were displayed of Saint Rocco, inseparable from his beloved dog, or Saint Francis who loved all animals. Only pet representations were welcome; the real things were banned. And to eliminate any possible doubt, next to the entrance of St Jakob's was a huge poster forbidding mobile phones, ice creams, shorts and crop-tops, cameras and, of course, dogs.

"It'd be quicker to say who *can* go in," said Etta sulkily. The trouble with owning a dog was that they had to visit almost everything individually, and it was nice to share experiences while chatting with your chum. And, of course, each visit to an attraction took twice as long, not to mention all the walks in parks and gardens, many times a day. Nope, it was time Miss Dorotea Rosa Pepe came to terms with the fact that Leon had to move on, before things got out of hand.

17

A CHASE ALONG THE TOWN WALLS

After another excellent dinner prepared by Dora, and after the washing and drying up had been done by Etta, the latter was happy to stretch out on the sofa and enjoy something as inconsequential as watching a little TV.

"I think the dog needs a short walk outside," Dora said.

"Oh, about that." Etta wondered for a moment if it was the right time to start the discussion about the dog and the need to find him a new home. But no, not now, it seemed. It was late, Dora was serene and relaxed, and Etta had a feeling her friend wouldn't be too pleased to deal with such a contentious topic. Evils – even necessary evils – were better discussed in the morning. "I'm a little tired, would you mind if I stayed home?"

"Not at all," Dora said, fetching the leash. Leon sprang up as if he'd been waiting the whole day for his five minutes outside, and Dora smiled at him while hooking the collar to the leash. "There's never enough of the outdoors for you, is there?"

Leon's nose fastened itself to the front door until Dora opened it, and then the two were finally out and about. Rothenburg was enveloped in darkness, broken by old-fashioned lamps shining their romantic yellow lights onto the cobbled streets, and there were hardly any passers-by. At night, this town was pure poetry.

Oh, the privilege of having a dog, thought Dora. *I would never have gone out all by myself at this hour if it weren't for Leon.*

Passing the Plönlein, they reached the Market Square. It was pleasantly empty, except for a couple walking along the far side. They were a little too distant for her to be sure, but Dora believed it was Charlotte and Johannes. But there was something odd about his bearing, something different that from a distance she couldn't put her finger on. She was about to call out to them, but she had the strange feeling that Johannes, on spotting her, had steered his fiancée towards the northern part of town, turning their backs to her and leaving the square.

Maybe they're just discussing something private, she thought, *and don't want to be interrupted.*

Both she and Leon decided to make the most of the empty square by taking a long walk all around it. Noticing details that, despite the darkness, were easier to spot now than when the square was full of tourists, Dora walked the full length of the Rathaus under the portico with Leon, and then from the opposite side of the square, she turned to admire its illuminated façade. Dora couldn't resist peering in the Christmas shop's windows, clasping her hands to her chest to embrace her emotion.

"Oh, Leon, imagine it! This year, we're going to celebrate Christmas in a real house." Her thoughts went back to the ugly flat she had left in Pietrapertosa when her friend and she had decided to share the expenses of Etta's pretty family home in Castelmezzano. It was a beautiful building, but to Dora, it was the equivalent of a real mansion.

"Woof!" protested Leon.

"Don't you worry, you're part of the family," Dora said as the dog pulled towards the Herrngasse. Dora wasn't too happy to go towards the Castle Gardens, especially alone at night. And under the influence of the late hour, she had the uncomfortable feeling she was being observed. The impression was so strong, she actually had to turn around and see if anyone was following her along the road. Although she couldn't see a living soul, the darkness, turns, porches, corners, thresholds meant it wouldn't take much for anyone to remain hidden from her sight.

Close to the city walls, she turned to glance back one more time. At that very moment, Leon pulled away. The next thing she knew, he was climbing up to the ramparts that run all the way along the top of the Rothenburg town walls, the leash click-clicking on the steps.

She called him back, but it has to be said that Basset Hounds, as cute and innocent as they look, are rather stubborn animals. Once he'd made up his mind to do something, Leon wouldn't change it. Ever.

Dora, as unwilling as she was, climbed the stairs after him.

"Leon, come here!" she whispered, projecting each syllable in a comic attempt to shout out without raising her voice. It wouldn't be a good idea to alarm the whole town with her screams, especially when all she wanted to do was to pass unobserved.

At least Leon wasn't running away; he just kept trotting along and looking back every so often to make sure that Dora wasn't too far behind. Fortunately, the covered rampart walkaways were partly illuminated. Although there were still a few too many shadows, at least she wasn't in total darkness, and the hound had enough white spots on his long body to make him visible. The dog was moving south, which meant they were getting closer to home – that was, unless she didn't manage to stop him before he'd done a whole circuit.

As Dora slowed down to catch her breath, she noticed stone plaques set in the wall to her right. She stopped to read the family names, remembering having learned that in order to restore the town, badly damaged by WW2 bombing, donations were asked of the public. Any sponsors who contributed to the repairs of a metre section of wall got a plaque acknowledging their contribution. There were local names, but lots of foreign ones too.

Leon, realising that he had somehow lost the attention of his biped, trotted back to her. Dora picked up the leash, but decided she'd better leave Leon free rather than risk being pulled over on the treacherous path. As for the dog, he was doing his best to make her understand it was time to go.

A sound rose from the middle of the town. Someone blew a horn, before crying, "It's midnight and all is well." It had to be someone in the Tourist Board's employ.

How nice, and how appropriate, thought Dora, her romantic side again coming to the fore. She lost herself, looking over the town roofs, a few windows still illuminated, imagining more than seeing the darkened shapes of the spires and towers that made up this atmospheric medieval fairy tale.

Dora stopped again to let it sink in. She bent to look through an arrow slit to the outside world, but the forest was so dark, she could only distinguish the lights of a few houses scattered in the distance.

Leon was getting more and more restless, coming and going to spur her on, and in the end, even Dora had to agree it was time to go. With Leon marching faster and faster, she was soon panting to keep up with him. And then she heard it, beyond any doubt.

Footsteps were following behind her.

Unable to utter a single word, she scuttled along behind Leon as quickly as she could. Not so easy in the dark of night, but she mustn't let fear slow her, neither the fear of the footsteps nor the fear of stumbling on the uneven stones under her feet.

She and Leon approached a lamp, but she didn't dare stop and look behind her. Instead, her eyes fell on Leon's back. Above his shoulder, his fur was bristling. He was just as aware as she was of the threat.

When would the long, windy passageway end? How far was the next tower with its stairs down to the ground? She couldn't sustain this speed for long, not even when the thought of a sharp halberd or a third shame mask sprang into her mind. Her spleen was crying out in pain, she had no more breath left and her heart was thumping wildly in her chest.

She heard a bang. Whoever was following her had stumbled or run into a stone, or done something that wasn't enough to stop them, but was loud enough to let her know they were far too close. Her legs were instantly paralysed. It was like a bad dream: it didn't matter how much she screamed at them to get moving, they wouldn't obey. She stood stupidly, immobile.

Is this the end?

Leon stopped abruptly, walked back to her. His friendly face had transformed. His ears back, lips contracted to show his teeth, hair prickling on his shoulders, he charged in the direction of the assailant, barking and howling louder than a thousand dogs.

In the houses all around, lights were switched on, shutters were opened, and people started shouting in a multitude of languages.

"Wer ist da?"

"Will you be quiet or I'm calling the police!"

"La gendarmerie, s'il vous plaît."

"Ci vogliono i carabinieri, che diamine!"

Leon kept barking. But neither he nor Dora could see anyone else on the ramparts.

The dog finally fell silent. Dora sighed heavily in relief, the oxygen seeming to reach her lungs and brain for the first time in a while, her blood pressure slowly readjusting to normal. She put Leon on the leash and invited him to follow her towards the tower. They took the stairs downwards and found themselves in a stone courtyard, tufts of grass growing from the illuminated walls. Passing under an arch, they were at the Plönlein. Home wasn't far.

∾

Etta was reading a book on the sofa.

"Are you still up?"

"So it seems. I couldn't sleep a wink," she said, hiding the fact she had wanted to wait up until Dora got back. "But what happened to you?" she added, noticing her friend's red face, the sweat on her forehead, the tangled hair.

Dora removed her jacket and collapsed on one of the armchairs in front of the green stube.

"Do you need a glass of water, or maybe brandy?"

"Water, please."

As she recovered, Dora told Etta what had just happened.

"My goodness! You risked your life."

"But Leon saved me."

"If it weren't for him, you'd have stayed safely at home," Etta replied icily. "We need to talk about him, but we'll do that tomorrow. As for today, I am intrigued. Who could have an interest in threatening you, and why?"

"Maybe it was just some silly youngster, thinking it's funny to frighten an old lady."

"With a killer on the loose, I'm much more inclined to think it was him or her."

"Maybe they saw us speaking with Luisa today?"

"That could just have been a random meeting. Unless… the TV!" cried Etta. "You remember what Luisa said? Everything you said to those journalists was shown on TV. The killer knows you intend to investigate the murders, and then he saw us talking to Luisa, and then… we don't know. Maybe he's spotted us speaking to other people, and when he heard you on TV, he knew for sure you're nosing around."

Etta walked towards the small guest room at the back of their house. Its window faced the Pfeiffers' home, and she could see the light on in one of the windows.

"I wonder if that's Johannes's room."

"You're not suspecting him, are you?"

"At this point, I'm not excluding anybody."

"Oh, come on." Now back in the cosy warmth of the house, Dora felt brave, even audacious.

"I'll tell you something. I came in here earlier to fetch one of my books." They had decided to use the spare bedroom on the ground floor as a store room for their empty bags and items that didn't fit in the upstairs bedrooms. "I'm sure all lights were off at the Pfeiffers' when you went out. Isn't it strange the light is on now? Whatever the case, we have to ask Marie which window is Johannes's."

"OK," Dora replied, feeling saddened. She liked Marie and knew more than anyone how worried she was about her son.

"And you didn't manage to see who was following you? Was it a man or a woman, tall or short, fat or thin?"

"I couldn't say, I never actually saw him or her. I was simply aware they were behind, following far too closely. And if it weren't for Leon…"

Leon raised his head proudly, looking from Dora to Etta.

"As I said, if it weren't for him, you'd have been lying in your bed since ten!"

Leon's head fell hopelessly to the floor. Was there no way to rescue this woman from her blindness? He'd be better off spending his time sleeping than trying to please her.

18

THE DOG SHELTER

After breakfast, Etta didn't waste any more time. She had to sort things out now. The peril her friend had faced the previous night had raised the need to prioritise security, but she had to weigh her words and arguments carefully. And being anything other than direct was not an easy task for her.

"Really, Dora, we should think about Leon. I spoke to Marie and she says the animal shelter is a wonderful place. There are lots of volunteers and they really love what they do, and they will find a proper family for Leon."

"But can't we simply keep him?" Dora's eyes had gone watery. Etta's words had stung her so badly, all her defences were broken down in an instant.

"I'm sure he's a better dog than I initially thought, but we still mean to travel, and dogs are animals of habit. They need a permanent home – where would we leave him whenever we stayed away for a month?"

"But he's adapted to our temporary home here in Rothenburg so easily…"

"There's a veterinary surgery at the shelter, we could ask for advice there. But if we are really thinking of carrying on with this trip of ours, and then going on the Mecklenburg home swap, we can hardly cram the dog on the backseat of the Fiat with all our luggage, and it's mean to expect him to live a nomadic existence. For all we know, they might not allow him in the house we'll be staying in. And on the way home, we'll need to book into a couple of hotels, and stay with your cousin in Trento. Wouldn't that be too much for the poor hound?"

Dora had always adored animals, but she had only managed, after a long quarrel with her reluctant father, to adopt one little kitten, who had stayed with her for 16 adorable years. She would love to share her life with a dog, but she had to admit that Etta had a point. Did she really know what was best for Leon? The only thing she knew for sure was that her heart squeezed in sorrow at the mere idea of being parted from him.

Reading her thoughts, Etta butted in quickly. "Anyway, we have an appointment to see the vet right now. And after we've spoken to him, we might as well take the chance to have a look around the shelter. We won't leave him today. But wouldn't it be wonderful if they found him a family while we were still in Rothenburg? You could visit him so he doesn't feel like we've abandoned him."

Hiding the few tears she couldn't hold back, Dora nodded, dropping her eyes to the floor. She didn't hug Leon as she longed to. No, she'd better not scare him by passing her distress onto him. She ran to the toilet to wash her face, blew her nose loudly and took a few minutes to compose herself. Then she was ready to show a happy face to Leon, patting him gently on the head – something the dog wouldn't usually allow, but he'd accept it from the roundish woman he had made it his duty to take care of.

"Well done, Dora," Etta said encouragingly, picking up her bag. "Let's go." But in her heart of hearts, she was fighting the uncomfortable feeling that behind all her logical arguments and rational thinking, something important had been left behind.

Leon walked alongside the two women, unaware of his fate and confident as ever, pretending to pee to incredible heights as if he were a massive Swiss Mountain dog, raising his leg, supple as a gymnast, and aiming for the treetops. Dora, on the other hand, was left unmoved by her surroundings for the first time since they had arrived in Rothenburg. She didn't stop at the Plönlein to imprint the image into her memory banks, nor did she gaze around the Market Square. Even the invitation to stop at the bakery for a schneeball couldn't tempt her.

After a long, silent walk through the modern part of Rothenburg, they found themselves facing a traditional building painted in a brilliant pastel blue. An iron gate had two bikes parked alongside it. They had arrived.

"Isn't it a cheerful, happy place?" Etta grinned encouragingly, but Dora's face was as merry as that of someone walking towards the executioner's chair.

A young woman asked if they had an appointment, confirmed the vet would see them shortly, and invited them to sit in an airy waiting room, the walls stencilled with dog and cat paw silhouettes. When they entered the room, Leon raised his ears suspiciously. He was familiar with this kind of place – the animal doctors often gave him nice treats, but they had an inappropriate habit of sticking a thermometer where the sun never shines. Humans were certainly odd creatures. Not too bad, if you didn't mind a few marbles missing.

Leon knew the vet and greeted him, allowing himself to be lifted onto the table for the usual unpleasantness to begin. He was an educated dog and bore everything with enormous patience, merely sighing every now and then.

"I believe our Leon is fine, he must simply have eaten something that disagreed with him," the vet said to Etta. "Give him these probiotics and carob-based pills twice a day for five days. Other than that, he's fit and healthy. I'm so glad he's found a new home so soon."

Dora looked at Etta in surprise. There was nothing wrong with the hound, so she realised that in order to book the visit,

Etta must have intimated on the phone that he had an upset stomach.

"Good to know." Etta smiled falsely. "But there is another reason why we're here," and she explained how they had only adopted the dog temporarily.

"I thought you were going to be Leon's new family," the vet replied without trying to hide his disappointment.

"That'd be lovely," Etta said, flushing slightly, which annoyed her, "but we wouldn't be a good fit for him. We travel a lot, so he'd have to spend months in dog kennels."

"Didn't you say you drove to Rothenburg?"

"Yes," Dora spoke for the first time. "We don't like flying, so we intend to drive everywhere."

"But that's fantastic! Then you simply take Leon on holiday with you."

Dora's eyes shone. Etta's face looked as if she'd been stung by a wasp, or maybe two.

"But dogs need a permanent home," she recited what she had read on the internet when preparing her speech for Dora. "They're animals of habit…"

"Nonsense!" The vet dismissed her words, shrugging his shoulders in a very canine fashion. "Dogs are natural wanderers. The only stability they need is their pack and a leader."

"But I'm sure I heard friends telling me how distressed their pets become when they go away on holiday…"

The man took off his glasses and invited them to sit in front of his desk.

"That might hold true for dogs who have either gone through some serious distress or had little socialisation and few life experiences, but Leon is a confident young fellow. He will love everywhere you go and will enjoy change just as much as you do."

Dora was in such a state of bliss, Etta could see her almost levitating into the air.

"But Leon is a distressed animal. Mr Sauer's neighbour told us how the man abused him…"

"Mr Sauer abuse Leon? Whatever are you saying, Mrs… Mrs…?"

"Passolina. Etta Natale Passolina."

"Mrs Pazzolina," the man tried his best to replicate the strange Italian 's' sound, "Sebastian Sauer simply adored his dog. He rescued him when he was an abandoned puppy, the runt of the litter, and never parted from him again – surely you have seen how well socialised and confident the dog is."

"I don't think you're right. When Leon joined our Night Watchman's tour, Sauer was mad at him. I'm sure he used to leave him home alone for hours and hours, which is as good as abuse for a dog."

The vet burst into loud laughter, annoying Etta even more. "There's some gold that does not glitter. Sebastian had a bad habit of trying to look worse than he really was. I can ensure you that Leon has taken part in every Night Watchman tour since the two became friends a year ago. Actually, more than friends." The man's small eyes met Etta's with an accusing look, or at least that's how Etta perceived it. "It's a special bond that ties a dog to his human. And it's not always a matter of choice. It was apparently by chance that Sauer found Leon, and now it's apparently by chance that Leon has found you. Never break that precious bond, Mrs Pazzolina; you'd never recover from betraying a dog's trust."

"I knew it!" The words exploded out of Dora. "This is why Leon has been searching for his owner, and is still looking for him. Mr Sauer loved his dog."

The vet nodded in approval. "By the way, is Leon eating his meals?"

"He ate almost nothing in the beginning," Dora said. "But he's taking a little more each day."

"It's a blessing you found him, and he found you," said the man, smiling kindly at Dora. Then he turned towards Etta and spoke to her gravely. "Take a look out of that window, Mrs Pazzolina. Yes, that one."

Etta went to the window overlooking a gravelled courtyard, watching volunteers taking the dogs from large cages and walking them round a fenced area, or playing games with them.

"The volunteers are doing a splendid job here for these sheltered dogs, madam, but the truth is every one of them longs for a real home. Don't give us another orphan, we've got plenty. It's likely Leon would soon be adopted, but that would mean one of the others would have to stay here longer, maybe for the rest of their life."

All of a sudden, Etta melted. It was as if a tide had been rising, silent and quick, catching her unawares. Before she knew it, she found herself held captive by an invisible enemy, fighting a war in which the weapons used against her were her own treacherous emotions and feelings. She flopped down on a chair; Leon went to sit in front of her and looked her straight in the eyes, his head tilted and waiting.

But he wasn't waiting for an answer. He wasn't asking, "Will you accept me or not?" but "Have you finally realised how things are? Was it necessary to put up all this fuss? Wasn't it clear from the start where this story was heading?"

"You've won," Etta blasted, "if that's what you want to know. And you too!" She glared at the dog, then at the vet, and finally at Dora. "Pay this animal doctor what we owe him and let's move on. We've wasted time enough."

But truth be told, when they walked back home in the shadow of the trees, the three of them side by side, Etta, for some inexplicable reason, felt so much better than when they had left home. But of course, she would never acknowledge that, not even to herself.

19

WATCH OUT!

U pon re-entering the town walls, Etta and Dora bumped into the chief inspector and sergeant. Despite the fact the police officers were clearly in a hurry, Etta stopped them to tell them what had happened the previous night when Dora had been chased up on the ramparts.

"That must just have been a figment of your imagination, Miss Pepe," the chief inspector dismissed their claims with a roar of laughter. "A murderer who's killed twice wouldn't be scared of that dog."

"That dog can become fierce if need be," Etta answered without hesitation. "And the possibility of being seen when half the town woke up probably had a helping hand in persuading him to desist."

"If you stop snooping around and stay indoors at night, you will be perfectly safe. This concerns Rothenburg inhabitants, not tourists who come and go. It's deeply rooted in local grudges."

"Local grudges, my eye!" Etta was not to be intimidated. "You'd better check what's going on at the Devil's Ale pub and the Goldene Traube. What are they trafficking? Drugs, weapons from Eastern Europe? Is that what you call local grudges?"

"Are you teaching me how to do my job?" The chief inspector drew himself up to his full height and looked down on Etta with an air of superiority, but it didn't take much of a stretch of the imagination to see that he was getting angry. The vein on the side of his head was pulsating visibly, his clean-shaven face getting redder and redder.

"Boss, didn't you mention you needed to get something for your wife at the local chemist," said the sergeant, pointing at the shop on the other side of the road, "before they close for their lunch break?"

In fact, it was almost two hours until lunch break, but luckily the chief inspector wasn't thinking clearly at that moment. The man looked around uncertainly, wondering if he still had to impose his authority on these two Italian hags. Then he looked at them with detachment, his face portraying how silly he considered getting into a discussion with gossips was, and finally a fear of returning to his wife empty handed prevailed. With a grunt, he turned on his heel and strode towards the shop.

As soon as they were alone, the sergeant asked for more information. Had Dora any idea who could have been following her? For how long did she believe she was followed? Had she spotted anyone she knew during her walk? Dora conveniently forgot that she had recognised Charlotte with what had looked like Johannes minutes earlier in the Market Square.

His mother lied to protect him, Dora thought, *now I'm holding back information on his behalf. Maybe this isn't the best idea…*

The sergeant handed both women her card. "In case of an emergency, do not hesitate to call me. But please, avoid going out at night. And don't go anywhere too isolated, at least until we have caught the culprit. The chief inspector is only worried for your own good. Though he might come across as harsh, he's right: there's real danger out there, and it may be closer than you think."

A frisson of fear went down Dora's back. Were she and Etta avoiding facing up to the truth?

"But now, off you go, he's coming back." The sergeant hinted towards the chemist's shop, and Etta and Dora hastened away. Neither the women nor Leon cared to speak to the man any more.

Once in town, they took it in turns to visit the Rothenburg Town Museum in a former convent. Dora adored the old cuisines and the romantic paintings; Etta learned about the history of the local Jewish community before it disappeared under the evil of the Shoah.

After the visit, Dora insisted on a celebratory meal in one of Rothenburg's restaurants. Usually, they were careful about eating out to save money for the rest of their travels, even more so now that Etta was finally considering the idea of a second house swap in the Mecklenburg region of a thousand lakes. On the other hand, the official enlargement of the family to include Leon deserved a little celebration.

After a glass of Tauber wine, a generous meal and an even more generous slice of dessert, they decided it was time to return home for a little rest. They were just crossing the Market Square when they came face to face with Johannes among the hordes of people cramming into the space.

"Are you going home?" he asked.

"Indeed we are," said Etta.

"Then we can walk together as far as the Plönlein. I'm heading to the pond to set up the outdoor exhibition."

Dora couldn't resist telling him the good news about Leon.

"I'm so glad!" the young man said, his clear-blue eyes smiling as much as his mouth. "I was hoping things would work out like this. I'm sure you'll do great together." He stopped to scratch the dog beside his ear. "Congratulations, Napoleon, I had no doubt you'd conquer these two."

And Leon bent his head towards the ground, finding being scratched just there irresistible. The guy knew how to treat a dog.

"Please, do tell Mum, she'll be so happy to know. If it weren't for our cats, I'm sure she would have adopted Leon; she was so worried you would drop him at the shelter, although I'd told her you couldn't possibly resist him."

"Such a lovely young man," said Dora as Johannes left them at the Plönlein.

"Sure, and Leon clearly trusts him, too," said Etta meaningfully.

THE REST OF THE DAY, THEY SPENT AT HOME. PART OF THE TIME, they pottered around in the garden, the rest of the time they were inside, poring over pictures of the Mecklenburg house on their laptop and reading the terms of the house swap. The owner would host them for a couple of weeks in their property, and in return asked them to have her younger son to stay in Castelmezzano for the month of August as he wanted to practise his Italian before starting college.

"The park, the rose garden, the orangery..." Dora's slate grey eyes were getting as large as her dreams. "And a traditional German wedding taking place while we're there – don't you think we should say yes?"

Dora and Leon looked at Etta, full of expectations.

"The house looks lovely," said Etta almost graciously. "Let's see if we can stretch our finances that far..." She didn't want to commit to the idea yet. Maybe it was too good to be true, and also, wasn't she being too agreeable with these two? Shouldn't she try to preserve some dignity?

Dora smiled as if she could understand everything that was going on inside Etta's mind.

"Don't you worry, Etta, we'll do what we can to save money. In the meantime, I'm going to prepare my bag, notebook and camera for tomorrow's Pretzel class. Are you sure you can cope with Leon while I'm away? I could ask Johannes and Charlotte to look after him in their shop until I'm finished..."

"Oh, don't bother. I guess the sooner I get used to the dog, the better."

20

THE BAKER'S SEAT

I t was past six o'clock when Dora came back from her cookery class. She had a box containing the fragrant pretzels with her and was impatient to show Etta. She couldn't wait to make them at home, too; she could already imagine the disapproving look of Zia Carmela, their neighbour back in Castelmezzano, who firmly believed the only edible dishes were the ones made according to the village traditions. But Dora was proud of her new skill, shaping the bread into a hug, or maybe someone praying. In fact, she had learned that pretzels were first made by a monk to celebrate Lent.

When she opened the door, Leon came wagging up to her, then he started to bark with such impetus, his front legs lifted from the floor and his ears flew in the air.

"Woof, Woof, Woof!"

It was a precise reproach for having left him behind. Dora laughed and looked outside; the sun was still high.

"Shall I take him for a short walk?"

"We had a walk in the Castle Gardens earlier this afternoon," said Etta.

The dog looked at her with a stupefied expression. "Have we

really been outside?" he seemed to be asking. "That must have been ages ago."

"I'll walk him for a bit. I want to see the pond Johannes said he'd be working on. I believe they've nearly finished that section of the outdoor exhibition now – do you want to come along?"

"I'm coming to the end of this murder mystery and am just about to find out who the villain is." Etta flipped her book. "Well, there are quite a few more pages to go, actually…"

"Then you carry on, we'll be back soon," said Dora, putting her box of pretzels on the small table next to the sofa where Etta was reclining. "And try one, please, they're perfect to accompany our soup tonight." Changing into more comfortable shoes, she took the leash from behind the door. Leon waited patiently until all the operations were complete, then his face lit up as if he was just about to be released into the outside world after years of imprisonment.

ETTA RAISED HERSELF TO A SITTING POSITION. THE BOOK STILL IN HER left hand, she pretended to read as her right hand made its way into the box of pretzels. But it would not do. She needed both hands.

She put the book face down, opened the box and instantly loved the smell that hit her nostrils. The pretzel was just perfect: lightly crunchy on the outside, and soft and fluffy on the inside, the grains of salt adding to the pleasure. She picked her book up again, adjusted the pillows behind her back, stretched her legs and continued reading.

Truth be told, she had half an idea who the villain was, but she knew from past experience that mystery writers don't play fair. Instead, they take a perverse pleasure in misleading their readers, encouraging them to suspect the innocent while disregarding the guilty. Etta was sure she had avoided a couple of red herrings, and surely she was on the right track now…

She took another bite of her pretzel before continuing.

~

OUTSIDE THE WALLS, THE COUNTRYSIDE ENVELOPED DORA AND LEON in the refreshing smell of cut grass and the soft lights of sunset. They descended towards the Tauber River and the red-tiled bridge. The small gravel path shone in the grass like the yellow brick road in the *Wizard of Oz*.

Dora let Leon run free as there were no passers-by and they were far from the road. He was happiness personified every time he discovered a new path or somewhere he hadn't been for a while. As he ran and sniffed, Dora spotted the part of the river where the Tauber created a pond. On one side, a wooden arm held a cage suspended above the waters. The lanky figure she saw working on the contraption must surely be Johannes, still trying to get this second part of the outdoor exhibition, situated outside Rothenburg's walls, ready for a few days' time.

"Hello," she called.

"Good evening," the man replied.

"Oh, good evening, Mr Winter, I thought you were Johannes." Dora reflected on how similar the two men were, both tall and thin with blond hair, especially when Mr Winter wasn't wearing one of his expensive suits or his distinctive bowler hat.

"Nope, he's gone home. Nowadays, producers, not to mention artistic directors, are supposed to be jacks of all trades, so here I am, the most humble of workers."

"Oh, you're such a tireless worker. And I think this is fascinating. We saw the baker's seat in the museum courtyard, but it's altogether a different thing to see it close to the water, where it was meant to be. Leon!" Dora called to the dog, who had evidently found something smelly that deserved his whole attention and was keeping his distance, deaf to the woman's entreaties. But at least she could see the white tip of his tail emerging from the grass.

Mr Winter joined her on the edge of the pond, next to the cage.

"Our medieval ancestors were such nice folk," he said sarcastically, nodding at the seat. "They knew exactly how to have fun in life."

"Mr Winter, don't be naughty! They took real pleasure in torturing people, but I guess education was still in its infancy. They didn't know about positive reinforcement. I say, isn't that Johannes' hat?" Dora pointed at a straw hat lying on the grass.

"The silly boy must have forgotten it. Will you take it back to him?"

"Of course I will," said Dora, bending to pick it up.

"Why don't you leave it there for a while? Don't you want to see how the baker's seat works?"

"You mean it really lowers into the water?" She put Johannes's hat down and looked again at Leon, who had started trotting towards them across the path. Then he stopped midway, another luscious smell demanding his full attention.

"It does." Mr Winter pointed to the iron pulley and handle close to him. "It's a good reproduction." As he started to wind the pulley, the seat lowered into the water.

"I wonder how deep it goes."

"As deep as necessary. If you were cheating people badly, they made sure you'd gurgle enough water into your lungs to teach you a lesson once and for all."

"That's a brutal punishment, even for a cheat."

He chuckled. "I'm only explaining how things worked in the good old days."

"Oh, please!"

"I'm not saying I approve of this manner of punishment either. But I must say, the cage is rather comfy."

As he said this, he raised the cage and pulled it back ashore. Opening the little door, he entered it.

"See? Large enough," he said, standing with his head lowered between his shoulders so as not to bang it against the top. "A good living space, perfect for spending a night."

Leon was trotting towards them once more. He was certainly a confident dog from his head to his tail, both of which were high in the air as if he was the master of his kingdom. But his smiley self-satisfied expression changed into something fierce – well, as fierce as a Basset Hound could look – as his eyes fell on the cage. He charged towards it, growling and barking, his hair bristling on his back. Mr Winter prudently stayed in the cage as Dora leashed the dog and tried to calm him down, but he was on a roll.

"Calm down, calm down! Good boy, there's nothing to be scared of," said Dora. Then she felt she needed to add an explanation to justify his behaviour to Mr Winter. "We had a bit of a fright last night…"

"Is he on a leash yet?" Mr Winter asked.

"He is, but you have nothing to fear. I guess he doesn't like the cage."

"Maybe if you were to show him it's not dangerous, he'd calm down."

"How should I do that?"

"Let me get out of here and I'll show you." Wolfgang Winter opened the cage cautiously. "You're sure he's on a leash, aren't you?"

"Completely sure." But Dora was experiencing some difficulty in holding the dog back, his fury giving his 30 kilos extra strength and impetus.

Mr Winter got out of the cage, held the door open and walked behind it so he was facing Leon through the bars.

"Walk him in," he said. "He will see there's no danger in a cage and will calm down."

Dora followed his advice. Overcoming Leon's resistance with gentle words, she pushed him until they were both inside the cage.

"You see, little doggy, that's all it is. Just a cage, not a ferocious dog. Nothing to worry about, at least not in this century."

But Leon kept barking and protesting with all his might. And when Dora turned around to exit the cage, she found the door closed. Mr Winter was further along the bank next to the wooden arm, working the pulley.

"Mr Winter, what are you doing?" Dora cried, finding it hard to be heard over Leon's barks.

"Don't you know? I'm getting rid of two nosey parkers who haven't been able to mind their own business from the very first moment they met."

21

TOO LATE!

"It was a rather theatrical murder," the detective inspector commented once the mystery was solved. Etta wasn't sure the book's conclusion had been particularly satisfactory, but those words kept dancing around in her mind, growing louder – so loud, in fact, that she dropped her third pretzel – or maybe her fourth? – back into the box.

Who had used similar words recently?

The shame masks came into her mind; not the ones she had seen at the Crime Museum, but those they'd found at the murder scenes. Dora! Yes, Dora had said the two murders were theatrical. Which was absolutely true. At times, it seemed to Etta that despite her acuteness, her cynicism making sure she was always ready for the worst, and despite Dora appearing to be a simple soul, a people pleaser, even a bit of a pushover, her friend had an ability to see through things, getting to the essence of problems. Theatrical, she had said. And that's exactly what the two murders were.

The halberd, the stocks, the shame masks…

An ordinary killer would simply have done their victims in and got on with their life as soon as possible. But this one had not only chosen a rather unusual weapon – a halberd – they'd also left a shame mask by each victim. But was that really the message the killer wanted to convey?

The two shame masks at the crime scenes pointed to the vices the two victims were guilty of, at least from the killer's point of view: nosing into other people's affairs and being a blabbermouth. But what if Etta was looking at this from the wrong direction? What if, rather than looking for the message behind the shame masks, she should be examining who had access to such unusual items? Who could obtain both the masks and the halberd with ease? The museum director, Mrs Fundstück, and her staff immediately sprang to mind, but there was also Johannes, who was responsible for the outdoor crime exhibition. But what if rather than being the murderer, Johannes was actually being framed?

The truth of the matter is, when you've been in a job for a long time, you start to operate automatically, no longer noticing that you leave your signature in the way you do things. Say it had been the Rothenburg Barbarossa behind the crimes. Their way of framing Johannes would have been totally different. Surely they would have dropped the murder weapon near his house, and they would probably have used a knife, not a halberd.

And what about the second murder? Who would think of leaving the bookkeeper in the stocks? Only someone who had a penchant for drama, in the literal sense of the word.

Etta stood up abruptly as if an electrical current had passed through her body, throwing the book to the floor. They had been misled by the silly dog. Leon had never shown any signs of intolerance towards the man as he had with the museum director…

Well no, wait a second. Leon had only met Mr Winter once at the bakery, and as the dog's arrival with Dora had coincided with Mrs Fundstück coming through the door, Etta had assumed he was barking at her. But what if…

And the second time Etta and Dora had met with him, the night of the play, Leon hadn't been there...

Goodness! Another thought drilled through her mind. At the Crime Museum, when Leon had met Mrs Fundstück for the second time, he hadn't reacted aggressively. In fact, he hadn't reacted to her at all. Etta and Dora had thought it was because he had neither seen nor smelled her, but what if the truth was that Leon was indifferent to the woman; that what he'd been trying to tell them in the café was that he didn't like Mr Winter, the theatre manager and artistic director?

A creative man with a sense of drama.

"I need to tell Dora straight away," said Etta out loud, grabbing her mobile phone, her heart thumping violently in her chest as the implications of her conclusion struck her. But no one answered the call, which after a few more rings went straight to voicemail.

"Those two! Why are Dora and Leon never here when I need them?" moaned Etta.

Then another thought flashed through her brain. Dora had implied during her TV debut that she was an experienced sleuth, and the killer hadn't wasted any more time – he had sprung into action that very night, following her along the town walls.

Or was Etta jumping to the wrong conclusion, trying to protect Marie and Joseph's son? After all, on the night of the chase, Dora had said she'd spotted Johannes and Charlotte... hadn't she? The lad could easily have been out and about when Sauer had been killed, and he certainly had been when Mrs Schilling had died, and when Dora had been in the Market Square before being chased along the ramparts.

Too many thoughts! Her head heavy, Etta dozed off for a couple of minutes. In her half dream, she imagined Johannes's lanky figure, walking ahead of her in the distance. But when the figure turned, it was Wolfgang Winter.

She awoke with a start, her mind lingering in the limbo between dream and reality, one single thought front and centre.

Johannes and Winter were both blond haired, tall and incredibly thin... they could easily be mistaken. It was only their clothing that set them apart. And Etta remembered the compliments Winter had showered on Charlotte, the huge bouquet of red roses she had been carrying after the performance of *Hamlet*. What if they had been from the theatre director?

Etta stood up; she couldn't risk dozing off again. She was at an important stage in developing her theory. Certainly, it was far from complete; she had no idea of the man's motives, for example. Why would Mr Winter want to kill Sebastian Sauer, to start with?

The cuckoo clock on the wall emerged to announce that it was 6.30. And suddenly, a feeling of dread seized Etta's mind, freezing all lucubration. What was it she had to do – urgently? Where did Dora say she was heading with Leon?

The outdoor exhibition at the pond. That was it.

After five o'clock, the streets of Rothenburg tended to clear of tourists, who would now be getting ready for their dinner. At 6.30, despite the sun still shining, you could be sure no one would be walking in the countryside beyond the town walls. No one would be close to the pond but Dora and Leon. They were alone, again.

Etta didn't like it. Once more she tried to call Dora, but again there was no answer. Should she tell the police? That chief inspector would laugh in her face as he had done with Dora, and possibly he'd be right. Still, Etta couldn't ignore her feeling of foreboding. She had the sergeant's phone number – the woman was definitely more friendly than her boss. Should she give her a try?

No joy. That call went straight to voicemail too.

What's the point of technology when everybody is determined not to use it?

As usual, Etta had to take the matter into her own hands. Actually, she'd better take something solid in her hands.

She went to the kitchen, snatched up a butcher's knife and

made for the door. In the hall, she caught a glimpse of her reflection in the mirror above the chest of drawers. It reminded her of Jack Nicholson in *The Shining*, so out of character for her, and she doubted she'd even be able to use the knife, no matter if she was facing a killer.

As she went back to the kitchen to drop the knife where she'd found it, she spotted a heavy wood and marble rolling pin in a small niche full of all sorts of cooking tools that Dora had used to make biscuits for the neighbours. She may lack in culinary talents, but Etta felt that was more her kind of weapon.

THE CAGE, LIFTED BY THE WOODEN ARM, SLOWLY MOVED OVER THE water's surface until it stopped in the centre of the pond.

"It was you on the town walls Sunday night!" cried Dora, understanding finally dawning on her.

"Maybe," replied the man infuriatingly.

"It was you who killed Sebastian Sauer! That's why Leon was growling and barking. It was you, not Mrs Fundstück, he was confronting when we met at the bakery!"

"Maybe."

"But the police will get you," Dora said, horror making her voice quiver slightly as the cage was lowered into the water, descending to wet her feet.

"That's where you're wrong, madam," he said with an apparently apologetic bow of his head. "Didn't you find Johannes's hat here just a couple of minutes ago?"

"So what?"

"So that's what the police will find too. We were working together earlier, Johannes and I. I hid his hat. But when they find you tomorrow, you and that insane dog drowned in the peaceful waters here, the police will call that hat evidence. And guess what? Your fingerprints are all over it too – 'proof' that you and the stupid lad were here together. Thank you kindly,

Miss Pepe, you've added the finishing touch to the perfect crime."

Dora had taken Leon in her arms. The water was now at waist level. He had his paws on her shoulders and was sending long, howling barks into the air. If only someone was around to hear them.

"The police will be here soon!"

"Not soon enough, madam. This is dinner time for German people and we take our meals rather seriously in this part of the world. In less than five minutes, it will all be over…"

The Tauber's waters, feeding the pond, were cold, but for Dora, struggling to keep Leon and herself above water, it was the cold of panic gripping her heart. What could she do? She had tried to wrestle the door open with her free hand, but it was well and truly locked. The shamed bakers of the middle ages would, of course, have tried that trick, too, and the cage had centuries of dipping experience to its credit.

Her free arm was now gripping the top of the cage in a last attempt to keep her head out of the water, but as the Tauber passed her chest and reached up to her neck, Dora knew her time had come. And she had involved poor Leon, too. The dog was still fighting for his life, whining and licking her face in turn.

"I hope it's not too cold, but I promise you it will be quick, if a little painful, maybe. Then I'll have to take care of your friend, making sure Johannes is implicated in her death, too."

The cage sank deeper and deeper, one centimetre at a time as the wooden arm overcame the resistance of the water. Dora was no longer shouting; both she and Leon were spluttering, gasping the last bit of oxygen available into their lungs, but the little air that was left to them was beginning to mix with water …

Faithful to her true self even in her last moments, Dora felt more sorry for the dear dog in her arms than she did for herself. She'd enjoyed more than 60 years of life; his was only just beginning. As she was saying her last prayers, the cage stopped, but she didn't even realise. She lost consciousness as slowly,

slowly, the cage rose into the air. The last thing she was aware of was Leon, coughing and squirming and trying to hold his beloved human up so she wouldn't drown in the water.

∼

"QUICK, QUICK, QUICK!" A WOMAN WAS SCREAMING ON THE BANKS of the pond, walking up and down and waving her arms in the air.

"You heard the lady, move faster!"

"B… B… Boss, I'm doing my b… b… best." The giant by the pulley was working as fast as he could, his face red and his biceps bulging. So huge was he that no one else could get near enough to help.

"Do better!" This came from a tiny bird-like woman with grey hair hanging straight to her shoulders, wearing a red scarf around her neck and black motorcycle leathers. Dwarfed by the tattooed man-volcano at her side, she was no less vocal.

"Heave ho, heave ho, heave ho!" The most notorious faces in all Franconia raised a chorus around the pond, beating their right fists against the palms of their left hands as they cried rhythmically.

"Come on, come on, he's killed them. My two dearest friends, I can't bear to lose them. Move faster! It's coming up, the cage is coming up. Be quick, be quick!"

The water was draining away, leaving the cage. And Etta could finally see Dora, her eyes closed, her back against the cage door, Leon licking her cheeks vigorously.

"My goodness, she can't be dead! She can't do this to me, leave me all alone. Quick, quick! I told you to be quick."

Blind to the menacing group around her and their unlikely companion of a frail elderly lady, Etta was shouting instructions to Otto, the huge man she and Dora had met outside the Devil's Ale pub. The poor man's sweat was beading on his bald head, the veins in his muscular neck straining against the red swords tattooed there; despite his strength, he was struggling to work the pulley as fast as he could, afraid it might be too late for at least one of the prisoners.

"Y… y… you ch… che… check on the man, missus. If he wa… wa… wakes up, he might try to repeat his g… g… game."

"I'll take care of him," cried the Boss of the Rothenburg Barbarossa, towering over an unconscious Mr Winter who was lying at his feet, the rolling pin Etta had used to hit the man minutes earlier on the ground a few centimetres away. "Come on, Auntie."

Had Etta been aware of anything other than the cage imprisoning her two dearest friends, she would have marvelled at the sight of the volcano who had so terrified her in the Devil's Ale pub extending a gentle hand towards the elderly lady in leather. With a glance at her Harley parked up nearby, Charlotte's gran – and, so it now appeared, the Barbarossa Boss's aunt – walked briskly towards him.

"But you, be quick," she shouted at Otto, jabbing a bony finger in his direction.

Finally, the cage was suspended above the water. Otto secured the main pulley and manoeuvred the wooden arm back to land.

As Otto opened the door and took hold of Dora, Leon jumped out, barking with less enthusiasm than usual, his ears low. He drew a figure of eight with his body, as if to say, "Please, do something to save this rotund lady of mine."

Gran, forgetting her watching role, walked over to help as Otto and Etta supported Dora's limp body, her brisk pace belying her age.

"My goodness, it's too late, she's dead!" Etta cried. Her friend was completely motionless as the man lifted her from the cage, lifeless as a corpse. With unexpected delicacy, Otto turned Dora on her side and moved her arms. A splurge of water came out of her mouth, followed by a number of coughs.

"She… she… she's alive," he stuttered, relief evident in his voice.

"She's alive," cried Etta hugging her friend.

"She's alive and kicking!" called Charlotte's gran, setting off a cacophony of discordant voices, their cheers echoing over the pond.

"Woof, woof, woof!" barked Leon, jumping around, wild with joy.

"I'm dead," whispered Mr Winter, slowly coming back to his senses, his head bursting with pain. His eyes opened briefly, widening as they recognised the Barbarossa Boss towering over him, a rolling pin in his hands. "I'm dead," he said again.

"What happened?" said Dora between a cough and a splutter, finally opening her eyes as Mr Winter's closed on the pain and the terrifying sight above him. Etta was hugging her and holding her upright.

"It's all over, Dora, everything's fine. You just gave me the fright of my life, that's all."

Leon kept dancing in circles, alternately growling at Wolfgang Winter and barking joyfully at his two humans. And when Etta hugged Dora, he put his head between the two of them, and Etta without hesitation kissed him on the nose.

"I love you, Leon," she cried. "I love both of you. Don't ever put your lives at risk again. Don't do this to me."

The Boss pulled a large white cotton handkerchief from his pocket with his free hand, his initials embroidered on the cloth by his beloved elderly aunt, and blew his even larger nose.

"Well done," he said, his voice hoarse. "Well done, Otto. We – the Rothenburg Barbarossa – will always protect the innocent, be they children, the elderly or our furry friends."

The rest of the gang of human bison launched into shouts of joy, all showing uncharacteristic signs of emotion on their ruddy faces, as Boss's aunt smiled her approval at his words. Otto wiped a tear away and hugged Leon, who had run to him to say thanks.

"Le... Le... Leon brings goo... goo... good luck wherever he g... g... goes."

And Otto was right. By chance, his motorbike had broken down in the proximity of the pond. Furious as he was at the dodgy components he had bought from Sebastian Sauer for his Harley, at first he'd hardly noticed the frantic barking of a certain Basset Hound, but by the time the rest of the gang, out for their afternoon ride led, as ever, by Charlotte's granny, had stopped to help him, Otto had acknowledged there must be a dog in distress somewhere. And it hadn't taken long before Boss had recognised the canine voice as belonging to Leon, a dog the whole gang knew and loved, despite his former master's trickery.

But now, the sound of sirens rapidly approaching came through the thickness of the forest.

"The coppers!" one of the human bison cried.

"Time for us to shove off!" roared Boss.

"What about Otto?"

"His bike is hidden from sight. He can jump on with Darby."

Otto high-fived Leon, then with the unexpected turn of speed of a rugby player running with the ball, he sprinted across the grass and climbed onto his fellow gang member's bike. By the time the police reached the pond, the area had been cleared and no one would have ever suspected a whole pack of bison had recently passed by. Only Charlotte's granny remained, standing by her Harley to make sure justice was established once and for all. With nearly nine decades to her name, she was above suspicion – just an innocent old hag with her marbles not all in the right place.

The detective sergeant had received Etta's message. She joined Etta and Dora, while the two policemen following her took hold of Mr Winter, lifting him to his feet and leading him away. As for the captive... well, he was surprisingly relieved at seeing that the terrifying Barbarossa volcano had been replaced by a couple of police officers, even if they were snapping handcuffs on to his wrists.

EPILOGUE

The next day, the detective sergeant called to visit the two women, finding them and their faithful Basset Hound in the garden in the company of the entire Pfeiffer clan. Marie had offered to cook lunch and take it next door so as not to tire Dora. Johannes was sitting beside his beloved Charlotte, while Joseph cast critical eyes over the garden and commented that he would mow the lawn the next day.

The most difficult thing for Dora had been to sit down and not prepare refreshments for her guests.

"Don't you dare!" Marie had scolded. "Leave it to me, I will do everything."

Etta, for her part, had no problem letting other people do all the work.

After the meal, when the sergeant popped by to ask how Dora was, she was offered a seat and a cup of coffee. There was no way she was getting away that easily – six pairs of eyes were looking at her for explanation. By tacit agreement, no one had mentioned the murders as they ate lunch, but now the time to tie up loose ends had arrived.

"Wolfgang Winter has confessed," the young sergeant said,

her lively dark eyes fixed on Etta. "But I have a feeling that Mrs Passolina here knows the whole story already."

Etta's cheeks turned as red as her hair, but she was clearly pleased with the compliment. Flattery didn't happen often enough in her life.

"Well, I can only assume…"

"Don't resort to false modesty, now," Joseph said, his smiling eyes softening his blunt words. "Spill the beans."

"Well, I never thought Mr Winter had anything to do with the murders until Dora's words came back to me. She had described the murders as 'theatrical', and yes, both murders were indeed rather peculiar. They weren't the style of the Rothenburg Barbarossa, for example, nor the rational Mrs Fundstück, even though the latter had access to all the unusual props we found at the crime scenes – the halberd, the shame masks. But the sense of the dramatic didn't match her personality at all.

"When the word 'theatrical' hit my mind, Mr Winter's image popped out of thin air. He's not only an original and creative man, but his sponsors, including the Fass family of the Goldene Traube, never seemed to raise enough money to finance his ambitions for the theatre. He said to me when we first met that I might like to become a sponsor, hinting that he was always on the lookout for financial backing.

"Then Marie and Joseph mentioned that the theatre received contributions from the municipality as well as private sponsors, so I started to wonder exactly how hard up the company really was. Compared to small businesses elsewhere, the theatre had plenty of backing, so did he really have reason to complain? So many supporters, but where was all the money going?"

"That's exactly what we concluded," the sergeant confirmed. "Winter has been embezzling incredible amounts money from the theatre. He was using the theatre credit card for his personal expenses, and he has rather refined tastes in travel, hotels, clothes. And some of the sponsors made their payments directly to him rather than into the theatre account."

"I'm not surprised," said Etta. "'Follow the money' has been our motto throughout the investigation, and remember that Mrs Schilling was the Rothenburg Theatre bookkeeper, too. I suspect in her position, she realised something underhand was happening to the funds. But rather than going to the police, she tried to blackmail Mr Winter. The suggestion she made to Johannes to evade taxes showed she wasn't above a bit of deceit herself. I feel confident that she not only knew about the money being embezzled, she'd also guessed who was behind Mr Sauer's death and her 'pay for silence' fee rose considerably."

"The poor Night Watchman," Dora said, patting Leon's head. "But why would Mr Winter want to kill Mr Sauer?"

"That's where we've been blind. We knew Mr Winter and Mr Sauer had argued, but we only had Mr Winter's word for it that it was about the Night Watchman's questionable working habits. I've a feeling, considering all his side hustles, Mr Sauer had found out what Mr Winter was up to, and he gave him an ultimatum: either return the money to the theatre funds or Sauer would tell the police."

"That's correct, Mrs Passolina," the sergeant nodded, "Mr Winter admitted to it. In fact, Mr Sauer knew how generous the sponsorship of the Goldene Traube was, and how many supporters the theatre had, so he couldn't believe that it was permanently in debt. Then he surprised Winter cashing in on some unsuspecting tourists and that's when he demanded Winter return all the money he'd stolen or he'd report him to the police."

"And *that's* when Winter planned the perfect murder," said Etta. "He knew where the tour would take Sauer, and he knew he'd pass Leon on to one of the guests for the duration of the tour. He knew tourists would fall behind at the Castle Gate, so he stoned the garden lamp early that morning, then waited for Sauer after nightfall."

"And the halberd?" asked Joseph.

"He'd been helping to prepare the Crime Museum's outdoor

exhibition, so Winter had free access to the museum's vaults. He 'borrowed' a real halberd, made sure the blade was as sharp as possible for when he needed it…"

"And the museum never noticed one of their weapons was missing?" asked Dora.

"No," the sergeant explained, holding her coffee mug with both hands as if enjoying the warmth emanating from it. "They only run an inventory yearly, and Winter was smart enough to steal one from the stores, not the exhibition. So they only noticed the halberd was missing when we asked them to check their collection after the first murder, to see if the murder weapon belonged to them."

"But in the beginning," Etta confessed, shaking her head, "all our suspicions were on either Johannes or Mrs Fundstück, who both had access to the weapon."

"You were one step ahead of us," said the sergeant, moving her eyes from the mug to Johannes and back to the mug again, as if to apologise. "We never really suspected Sophia Fundstück as we'd fixated on poor Johannes here."

Indifferent to the detective sergeant's apologetic glances, Etta carried on. "Winter killed Sebastian Sauer using the real weapon and took away the fake halberd; his sense of the dramatic would never allow him to leave two weapons at the murder scene. In this respect, he was a… shall we say, professional?"

"And was the shame mask from the museum too?" Charlotte asked.

"No, that was a copy," the sergeant said. "It's stocked in many of Rothenburg's shops – including yours, I believe – and of course, that implicated Johannes even more. As a shopkeeper, he had free access to this kind of merchandise…"

"And to seal my fate," said Johannes, "he repeated all this with Mrs Schilling's murder."

"Yes," Etta confirmed. "His timing was perfect, too, as we had all witnessed your row with her after the performance of *Hamlet*."

"What I don't understand," said Dora, glancing at the sergeant as if wondering whether she should mention the issue or not, "is what was going on between the Devil's Ale pub and the Goldene Traube?"

"That's simpler than you may think." The sergeant looked at Etta. "Can you answer this one, too?"

Etta was always eager to accept a challenge. "Am I wrong in suspecting that Martin Fass and the waiter, Tony, had started a trade in cannabis, which had – unbeknown to Martin's parents – become one of the crops growing in the Fass family's fields?"

"No, you're not wrong. Weed is illegal in this country, but Tony and Martin figured out, using the reputation of the Rothenburg Barbarossa and the respectability of the Goldene Traube as cover, they could make a good profit with their criminal commerce."

"I still don't understand the role of the Rothenburg Barbarossa," Marie said.

"In fact, they have no role," said Etta, "except as a sort of lightning rod. With memorable faces like theirs all around, one would hardly notice Tony, a plain waiter with no distinguishing features. We were imagining the Barbarossa were involved in weapons trafficking, heroin smuggling; who would ever have suspected a simple waiter of trading in hashish?"

"And Martin's parents?" After all Johannes had gone through, Marie found it hard not to sympathise with them.

"It has been a harsh blow for them," the sergeant said, sitting on the edge of her chair to give gravity to her words. "But you know, it's better we caught the young man now, rather than later when he might have got involved in something much bigger and more dangerous. It's an easy step from weed to Class A drugs once you're in the circle. I hope the dude will realise that his family business and hard work are the best future he can wish for."

"So the Rothenburg Barbarossa are…"

"As innocent as little lambs."

"And how about Mrs Fundstück?" Dora asked.

"Nothing on her, either." The sergeant sat back in her chair again. "Frankly, I couldn't figure out why you were so hostile towards her."

"But Leon was barking at her…".

Etta interrupted Johannes. "Just like you, she was the wrong person in the wrong place at the wrong time." She could now see the implications of everything she had discovered. "The wrong person because she's so easy to dislike, the wrong place and time because her arrival at the bakery coincided with Leon's so we thought he was barking at her, when in fact it was Mr Winter who had upset him. Leon surely recognised the man's smell from the Night Watchman's corpse."

"Do you think Winter was still around when Leon ran over to Sebastian's body?" Johannes asked.

"I think he would have disappeared instantly, but his smell would have lingered. And Leon would have been present when they argued and Sebastian threatened to tell the police the truth about Winter's crimes. The dog must have sensed the threat in the air. We can call it a Basset hunch."

"That would explain a lot of things," said Dora. "The vet at the shelter told us Mr Sauer was not that bad, and that he really loved Leon…"

"He was even better than that," said Johannes, standing up to break his news to his family. "The Tourist Board have called me up to be the next Night Watchman. Mr Sauer had already told them this was going to be his last season; he wanted to get a little money behind him before leaving the field to a younger man, and apparently he'd put my name forward. He'd even said I would be perfect for the role. I can't believe I held such a grudge against the poor man…"

They all clapped their hands and hollered and cheered for Johannes, holding their coffee cups high and clinking them together.

When the shouts died down, Dora said, "He was indeed

made of gold that does not glitter," recalling the words the vet had used. Looking at Etta, she wondered if her friend and Mr Sauer didn't share quite a few traits in common.

"But why would Wolfgang Winter try to frame me?" asked Johannes, sitting down again and taking Charlotte's hand.

"That's a very silly question, young man." Although Etta reproached him, she was glad he had given her the chance to escape Dora's stare. "Not only did he need a scapegoat, but he had lost his heart to your fiancée…"

"It's true," Charlotte said, her already rosy cheeks flushing. "The awful man tried to seduce me. He sent me flowers and told me what a good actress I was, and that I should think of making it a profession rather than a hobby. On Sunday after the second show, he insisted on accompanying me home, said I should find a soulmate, someone who could understand my artistic talent…"

"Wait a second," Etta jumped in. "On Sunday night, you were with Mr Winter?"

"I was," replied the girl, startled. "Why?"

"Did you and he not see Dora and Leon in the Market Square?"

"I don't think so…"

"I do. At least, he did. Tell me, did he leave you as soon as he'd accompanied you home?"

"As a matter of fact, he did. He was in the middle of complimenting me, and then all of a sudden, he wanted me to hurry home, and he didn't even wait to see me to the door before he was off…"

"Yes, off to chase Dora and Leon on the ramparts."

"I've been so silly," and Charlotte nestled her little face against Johannes's shoulders. "I never so much as kissed him, but I was flattered by his words. Can you forgive me?" She could hardly look him in the eyes.

Johannes lifted her chin and kissed her sweetly as all the others pretended to look elsewhere.

THE GUESTS HAD LEFT AND DORA HAD GONE TO SLEEP, AND THE moon was shining peacefully over Rothenburg. Only Concetta Natale Passolina was lingering in the garden. She still had too much adrenaline running through her body to go to sleep.

She had a book in her hands about German culture, but she wasn't actually reading; she was brooding over the latest events in her life, trying to make sense of them. The choice to invite Dora to live at her place in Castelmezzano, and then Dora's crazy idea of travelling throughout Europe in a Fiat 500 on a series on nonsensical home swaps had turned her life upside down. Well, actually she had to acknowledge it had worked remarkably well so far. Much better than she had ever expected; in fact, so well that they were due to leave lovely Rothenburg ob der Tauber in a couple of weeks' time and head for the Mecklenburg region in the north-eastern part of the country – the land of a thousand lakes. They had been invited to attend a traditional German wedding – the son of the home swap hosts was getting married in a beautiful mansion surrounded by gorgeous parkland. Imagine that!

Etta was dreaming of stunning countryside and glamorous guests when a low "GRUMPH" rose from under the table in front of her. Her heart thumping, she slowly bent to check what was going on.

Napoleon was there, fast asleep, growling at imaginary enemies, his body twitching and jerking, his paws moving in the air as if running with a hunt. She hadn't realised the Basset Hound had stayed to keep her company. Lightly touching his shoulder, she woke him as gently as possible, and when Leon raised his head, she invited him to follow her inside.

As the door closed behind them, Etta whispered, "Don't you worry, little dog, we're going to have lots more fun and adventures together. It seems that even in retirement, life can still be full of surprises."

A WEDDING AND A FUNERAL IN MECKLENBURG

A GERMAN COZY MYSTERY

A Wedding and A Funeral, in Mecklenburg is the second book in the *Homeswappers Mystery* series.

TO BE RELEASED ON 15 OCTOBER 2020

PREORDER ON AMAZON NOW

Weddings can be Murder

Retired teachers, Etta and Dora, continue their homeswapping adventures across small European towns in their yellow Fiat 500.

Their latest journey leads them to a beautiful mansion in Mecklenburg Pomerania, the Land of a Thousand Lakes in Northern Germany.

Excited at having been invited to their homeswappers' son's wedding, Etta and Dora would never have expected to witness one of the wedding party dropping into the wedding cake... dead!

With the help of Leon, their basset hound, and his heart-melting skills, Dora's charm and intuition, and Etta's sharp mind, the three sleuths set out on the trail of the murderer.

But does that road lead to grave danger?

[Final Blurb to Come]

PREORDER ON AMAZON NOW

MORE BOOKS FROM ADRIANA LICIO

THE HOMESWAPPERS SERIES

0 - Castelmezzano, The Witch Is Dead – Prequel to the series

1 - The Watchman of Rothenburg Dies: A German Travel Mystery – coming on the 1st September 2020

2 - A Wedding and A Funeral in Mecklenburg : A German Cozy Mystery – coming on the 15th October 2020 - **Preorder Now**

3 - An Aero Island Christmas Mystery: A Danish Cozy Mystery – coming on 1st December 2020 - **Preorder Now**

AN ITALIAN VILLAGE MYSTERY SERIES

0 - And Then There Were Bones. What better than an invitation for a murder mystery week-end on a sunny Calabrian Island? Or maybe not? *And Then There Were Bones* is the prequel to the *An Italian Village Mystery* series, and it is **available for free by signing up to www.adrianalicio.com/murderclub**

1 - Murder on the Road Returning to her quaint hometown in Italy following the collapse of her engagement, feisty travel writer Giò Brando just wants some peace and quiet. Instead, she finds herself a suspect in a brutal murder.

2 A Fair Time for Death is a mystery set during the Autumn

Chestnut Fair in Trecchina, a mountain village near Maratea, involving a perfume with a split personality, a disappearing corpse, a disturbing secret from the past and a mischievous goat.

3 - A Mystery Before Christmas A haunting Christmas song from a faraway land. A child with striking green eyes. A man with no past. A heartwarming mystery for those who want to breathe in the delicious scents and flavours of a Mediterranean December.

4 - Peril at the Pellicano Hotel – A group of wordsmiths, a remote hotel. Outside, the winds howl and the seas rage. But the real danger lurks within.

ALSO

"When The Clock Chimes Two" a short story in *"Mystery Follows Her"* a collection of intriguing and light-hearted stories by nine award-winning and best-selling authors from across the globe. My own story features Giò Brando, Agnese and a mischievous perfume with a mesmerising name "Passage d'Enfer". It can be a good introduction to my *An Italian Village Mystery* series.

"Life Lines" a three-page story featuring Giò Brando and her Grandmother in **"Stop the World: Snapshot From a Pandemic"** 40 authors from around the world set out to record their innermost feelings -- to offer inspiring, heartfelt, creative takes on the Covid-19 pandemic. Crime fiction, elegant and angry poetry, and gut-wrenching personal essays: all paint a picture of the year and help us make sense of the sacrifices we've made in 2020.

AUTHOR'S NOTE

Rothenburg ob der Tauber

I've tried my best to describe the enchanting town (almost!) as it is. During my visit with my husband and dog (it was a short stop between a home swap in the German Alps and another in Hamelin), we stayed in a pretty guesthouse. Suffice to say, I fell so much in love with both our temporary residence and the town, I had no trouble imagining what a home swap there would be like.

The young couple who ran our guesthouse were hospitable and kind, and I overheard – not that I would ever eavesdrop on any conversation, you understand – the wife telling her husband to trust in himself more, and that comment was the inspiration behind the characters of Johannes and Charlotte. On the morning of our departure, we found out the battery of our car was flat, and our generous hosts helped us out with that. They provided splendid food in their restaurant, but every time we sat down to order our meal, the first one to be served (both water and fresh food) was Frodo, our golden retriever. As a result, it was relatively easy for me to imagine how Rothenburg folk would behave towards Leon, the loveable Basset Hound of our story.

The Night Watchman

In Rothenburg ob der Tauber, there really is a Night Watchman, and his name has passed on to legend as he's been guiding tours for the last 25 years, becoming an unmissable Rothenburg attraction for those smart enough to stay for at least one night. This legend's name is Hans Georg Baumgartner, and if you ever visit Rothenburg ob der Tauber, do not skip his night tour. Not only is it informative and fun, but Hans Georg has the good sense *not* to get killed while waiting for his guests. In 25 years, he's never caused any of the troubles Etta and Dora went through.

My Rothenburg Watchmen, both old Sebastian and young Johannes, bear no resemblance whatsoever to the real Watchman; they're just a product of my imagination. And all the references to an agreement with the Rothenburg Tourist Board are equally fictitious – just a ploy to fuel the story.

Elizabeth Peters *Borrower of the Night*

In the book, Dora mentions a mystery novel set in Rothenburg ob der Tauber called *Borrower of the Night*. Featuring art historian and amateur sleuth Vicky Bliss, it was written by Elizabeth Peters, one of the pen names used by Egyptologist and mystery author Barbara Mertz. It's a clever whodunit, and I recommend reading it if you want to linger in Rothenburg just a little longer. In fact, I'm so charmed by this town, I might send Etta and Dora back for Christmas.

I couldn't find any other books in English set in Rothenburg. If you come across any, then please drop me a line.

Home swapping

In 2005, Giovanni, my hubby, mentioned that we (both being travel freaks) should join a home-swapping association so we could travel more often and see places in a different light. At the time, I didn't pay much attention. The idea of having 'strangers' wandering about my home held no attraction for me.

But he tried again and again. If I'm stubborn, Giovanni's even more so. He turned up in my perfumery with a friend of his, a teacher from Padova who has literally travelled the world using home exchange schemes. She has two girls, and they have been travelling with their parents since they were babies.

Has she ever found her home disrupted on her return? Never in more than 40 home swaps.

Has she made new friends? Plenty.

Doesn't she find hotels are more comfortable? No, they are less personal. She has come to loathe the very idea of spending her holidays in a hotel.

The next day, I called Annalisa, an amazing woman and the President of the Italian branch of an international home swap organisation. She had organised something like 150 successful home swaps, and by then had a real sense of belonging to the world. Her two children had been brought up by countless different families, because yes, you can also swap children if you're fed up with your own…

OK, I'm kidding, but under the scheme, you can host a family's child, and then have the favour returned.

With home swapping, for a weekend, a week, a month, you don't spend a small fortune to stay in an anonymous hotel with thousands of other tourists; you become part of the local community, staying in a family house that's typical of the area. You use their bikes (or kayaks), you're given directions to the local markets, the best bakeries, the most exciting activities in town, the tiny restaurants that never make it into a tourist guide. And more often than not, you get invited for a cup of coffee, an aperitivo or even dinner with your new neighbours (who have been duly informed by your hosts).

Two months after my talk with Annalisa, we were staying in a splendid riad in the Marrakech Medina. We have travelled to Vancouver Island, Berlin, London, Hamelin (the town of the Pied Piper), and then in 2009, Frodo, our adventurous golden retriever, joined the family. To my utmost surprise, we've never had to house the jolly beastie in dog care while we take a holiday. We just gave up flights and started to drive all the way from down, down, down the Italian boot to Sweden, Great Britain, Switzerland, Brittany, Slovakia, the Pyrenees and many more places.

It's now 2020 and the Coronavirus pandemic is sweeping the globe. This will be the first year since 2005 that we won't house swap with anyone, so I've handed the baton to Etta and Dora and am enjoying my armchair travels as much as I hope my readers will. And this is only temporary; I'm waiting for the day we'll be able to hit the road again.

ABOUT THE AUTHOR

Adriana Licio lives in the Apennine Mountains in southern Italy, not far from Maratea, the seaside setting for her first cosy series, *An Italian Village Mystery*.

She loves loads of things: travelling, reading, walking, good food, small villages, and homeswapping. A long time ago, she spent six years falling in love with Scotland, and she has never recovered. She now runs her family perfumery, and between a dark patchouli and a musky rose, she devours cosy mysteries.

She resisted writing as long as she could, fearing she might get carried away by her fertile imagination. But one day, she found an alluring blank page and the words flowed in the weird English she'd learned in Glasgow.

Adriana finds peace for her restless, enthusiastic soul by walking in nature with her adventurous golden retriever Frodo and her hubby Giovanni.

Do you want to know more?
Join the **Maratea Murder Club**

You can also stay in touch on:
www.adrianalicio.com

facebook.com/adrianalicio.mystery

twitter.com/adrianalici

amazon.com/author/adrianalicio

bookbub.com/authors/adriana-licio

THANKS

Every new book is an adventure, but a new series is the adventure to end all adventures!

Thanks to all my readers, who welcomed an unknown author from a remote area of Southern Italy (it's called Basilicata, by the way) and gave my *An Italian Village Mystery* series such a warm reception that here I am, writing more. It's due to your huge support that this new series is happening, and I do hope you will enjoy reading it as much as I'm enjoying planning and writing it.

Thanks to my wonderful, heroic editor, Alison Jack, who jumped on board with this mad enterprise and is learning Italian faster than I improve my English. As she corrects my notes on Maratea, it seems she knows the place better than I do.

Thanks to Dar Albert, my cover designer, who magically makes sense of my briefs hinting at a thousand and one impossible things to come up with one brilliant cover after another.

Thanks to the indie authors' community in general and the Alliance of Independent Authors in particular, all so helpful and encouraging. I've learnt a lot in the past three years and continue to learn from you all.

Thanks to my family who not only support me and my creative madness as my writing takes me elsewhere, but keep trusting me whatever I do. Love you all!

Thanks to my tireless and enthusiastic beta readers who help me to spot issues in my manuscripts and give me invaluable feedback on all I write.

Printed in Great Britain
by Amazon

84984948R00103